Wintersong

MICK LOWE

Wintersong

THE NICKEL RANGE TRILOGY • VOLUME 3

Baraka
Books

Montréal

© Mick Lowe

ISBN 978-1-77186-106-9 pbk; 978-1-77186-116-8 epub; 978-1-77186-117-5 pdf; 978-1-77186- 118-2 mobi/pocket

Book Design and Cover by Folio infographie
All illustrations including cover: Oryst Sawchuk
Editing and proofreading: Barbara Rudnicka, Robin Philpot

Legal Deposit, 2nd quarter 2017
Bibliothèque et Archives nationales du Québec
Library and Archives Canada

Published by Baraka Books of Montreal
6977, rue Lacroix
Montréal, Québec H4E 2V4
Telephone: 514 808-8504
info@barakabooks.com
www.barakabooks.com

Printed and bound in Quebec

Société de développement des entreprises culturelles

Québec

We acknowledge the support from the Société de développement des entreprises culturelles (SODEC) and the Government of Quebec tax credit for book publishing administered by SODEC.

Financé par le gouvernement du Canada
Funded by the Government of Canada | Canada

Trade Distribution & Returns
Canada and the United States
Independent Publishers Group
1-800-888-4741 (IPG1);
orders@ipgbook.com

Contents

PART THREE
Early Spring

PART FOUR
Late Spring

Mick Lowe (Oryst Sawchuk, 2017)

To the women—and men—of '78-9

"Revolution is the workers' festival."
—V.I. Lenin

The author gratefully acknowledges the contributions of David Patterson, Cathy Mulroy and Jim Gordon for their contributions to this book, as well as to the courageous sacrifice and solidarity of the thousands of Sudbury men and woman who inspired this story. These men and woman could not be broken by any force that attempted to conquer or divide them for 261 days. The author hopes that this book will help make their story be known to future generations.

PART ONE

Fall

1

"Out 'til the Grass is Green!"

Sudbury, Ontario, Canada
September 15, 1978

Like all good movies, this one begins with a song.
It was everywhere that fall and late summer, rattling out of the tinny speakers of cheap transistor radios in truck-stop kitchens, booming out of two-ton Wurlitzer jukebox woofers in every honky-tonk bar north of the French, always sung with a Nashville twang as coarse and unadorned as a rasp file: "Take this job and shove it! I ain't workin' here no more!"

It was seen by all of them as their song, telling the story of their lives, their theme song. And they would, in their thousands, have flipped the company the bird as they strode through the plant gates that end-of-shift, except both hands were full, as they lugged their belongings and dirty laundry from cleaned-out lockers.

Nearly twelve thousand hard rock miners and nickel smelter and refinery workers left the plants with swagger that night: "Take this job and shove it!"

They were pulling the pin, "Stickin' it to the Man." Greeting their departing comrades, they brimmed with a bravado their wives might not have shared, thinking of their children with no Christmas, and cash running low over the long winter months ahead: "Out 'til the grass is green, brother!"

Fuckin' A! "Out 'til the grass is green!"

They were like lemmings, piling off a high cliff, about to plunge to their own mass graves, all the papers and politicians said so, even the political leaders of their own, social democratic party, the party of the workers. Hell, even some of their own union leaders said it. "Do Not Strike: Union Leader" was the skyline headline blazoned page one above the flag in the province's largest circulation daily newspaper.

And they all knew it was true: they were taking on a ruthless and enormously rich opponent, one they had strengthened by letting their own stupidity and cupidity crowd out common sense by creating a huge stockpile, more than three million pounds of finished nickel—enough to last the company a year without an ounce of additional production—in their eagerness to make money through overtime work and the bonus system.

But there was also a strategic component to their mindset, a nuance largely overlooked by the news media of the day: despite turning a handy profit the previous year, the company had laid off several thousand of their co-workers, made effective just the previous February. Odds were, still more layoffs were on the way. But maybe, just maybe, a bold counter measure, a counter-intuitive move like a seemingly suicidal strike, might forestall further layoffs. All would sacrifice to save the lowest-seniority-and-youngest few. An injury to one . . .

So maybe they were like men waiting for the trap door to swing. Fuck it! They were young, many of them, and they were cocky. "Take this job and shove it! I ain't workin' here no more!"

"Out 'til the grass is green, brother!" the old guys swore, fists upraised.

"Out 'til the grass is green!" the young guys nodded with knowing smiles.

2

Disarmed, Still Dangerous

Jake McCool ran his hands through his dark, tousled, slightly curly hair. He was tired now, there was no doubt about it. The buzz he'd received from the spliff he'd shared with his wife Jo Ann hours ago, and which had supercharged the adrenalized emotions they both felt at the prospect of an imminent strike by thousands of Jake's co-workers at Inco Limited, the largest nickel-producing company in the world, had long since worn off. These were dangerous times, and they both knew it. The dope rush had sharpened that edge, but it had ebbed during the long overnight hours.

As he cradled the phone, Jake exhaled a long low sigh, equal parts relief and weariness. He'd just spoken with the last picket captain on his list— Tommy Flanagan, out at the Number One Gate of the smelter in Copper Cliff. Flanagan, a longtime shop steward at the enormous smelter complex, reported that a picket line was up—had been since midnight, when the old contract expired. The line was well manned by forty or so union stalwarts spoiling for a fight.

"Some of 'em are pretty well oiled, Jake, been drinkin' all night," Flanagan had confided with a hint of amusement in his voice.

"Yeah, well, just keep 'em dangerous but disarmed, Tommy," Jake replied. Both men laughed at this reference to the '66 wildcat, when someone on the smelter line had fired several rounds with a high-powered hunting rifle at the helicopter ferrying management personnel in and out of the strike-bound smelter complex. A direct hit would have been disastrous, except that the liquored-up striker who'd pulled the trigger couldn't hit even one of the three choppers he'd seen through his sights. But the muzzle flashes had alarmed the pilot, a Korean War vet, who radioed them in immediately, a report which promptly led to the mobilization of hundreds of provincial police who were immediately dispatched to Sudbury to quell any threat of civil unrest from the fourteen thousand or so pissed-off nickel workers who had suddenly staged a massive, spontaneous—and illegal—walk-out at Inco's sprawling operations across the Sudbury Basin.

Both Jake and Flanagan had laughed at the light-hearted reference to the wildcat of '66, but both were acutely aware they were sitting on a powder keg—the roiling, incessant resentment of a hard-boiled rank-and-file towards an employer that had bested them in bargaining and strike situations time after time, resulting in successive post-strike returns to work with a residue of sullen resentment and simmering rage that had only accumulated over the decades. The legal strike over which they were presiding and which was now a scant six hours old was about all that, both men knew. Across the Basin knots of angry men were now gathered around oil-drum fires fed by the greasy, highly combustible creosote of torn-up railway ties. They were wild men now, wild and hungry for payback, freed from the fetters of the workaday world and the discipline of the workplace. Booze was common, and occasionally an empty beer or liquor bottle would be launched, whizzing high through the night air, towards company property, usually smashing harmlessly into the empty parking lot accompanied by the distant, soul-satisfying sound of breaking glass. Even that small gesture, a precursor, perhaps, of greater mayhem to come, was greeted with a rousing, ragged cheer.

The first gray light of dawn was just seeping in under the drawn blinds of Jake's Steel Hall office as he hung up the phone.

So. That was that. The largest integrated nickel mining-milling-refining operation the world had ever seen was now well and truly idled, every mine and plant entrance blockaded by Jake's fellow union members, each picket line led by union activists Jake knew and trusted, three hand-picked captains to rotate through the three eight-hour shifts. Like the surface plants they now had a chokehold on, the picket lines would be a continuous operation, manned night and day for the foreseeable future.

Jake rose wearily from his desk and walked the few paces to his office door.

"Done deal, Ang," he announced to Angel Houle, his secretary, whose desk was just outside his office door. "All lines are up. Just got off the phone with Tommy Flanagan out at the smelter. We've got the whole shebang tied up tighter'n a tick."

Houle's brown eyes widened. She was the youngest secretary on the floor, a new hire, and Jake liked her for her energy, her enthusiasm, and, most of all for her great good humour, which bubbled up through her demeanour like a tireless, never-ending artesian spring.

"No rest for the wicked, though, boss," she responded, glancing at her wristwatch. "Jordan's called a meeting for nine o'clock sharp."

Jake nodded mutely. Not for the last time in the coming months, Angel was giving *him* orders, telling him where to go and when to be there.

Three hours. Just enough time for a pick-me-up at his favourite coffee shop.

3

Council of War

Jake hopped in his car, and pointed it north, through the Flour Mill district, toward Lasalle Boulevard. The route took him through downtown, where the streets would normally be jammed at this time of day, with day shift workers hurrying to their jobs at the smelter and refineries west of town. But today, with the strike on, traffic was noticeably lighter. Jake's destination was a newly opened coffee shop at the corner of Lasalle and Montrose.

Despite its odd name—for a defenseman for the Toronto Maple Leafs who'd died recently in an automobile accident—the place had quickly become a favourite of Jake's. He just flat-out loved their coffee.

As usual, the place was bustling, even at this early hour. Jake was lucky to find a table. He couldn't help but hear snatches of the animated conversations that swirled around him. Clearly the strike was the subject of the day, and the place was alive with rumour and speculation. The buzz was so palpable that Jake could almost taste it, along with his first sip of the bitter, scalding hot black coffee that was so highly caffeinated that Jake knew it would give him a coffee jag of sufficient strength to offset his fatigue and carry him through the day ahead.

The air around Jake was alive with excitement, a keen anticipation over what would come next. It was, Jake reflected, almost a sense of liberation. He wondered how long that would last, once the novelty of the situation had worn off, and the monotony of life on the picket lines, with winter setting in, had become the new norm?

Still, the buzz was infectious, and it, plus the coffee, propelled Jake, with lifted spirits, back to the Steel Hall.

The mood was different inside the union hall, where he found Jordan Nelson, somber at the gravity of their situation, already sitting at the head of the boardroom table, waiting impatiently for the others to file in. As usual, the President of Local 6500 was all business. Like Jake. Nelson was barely thirty, a precocious age for a strike leader to be entrusted with such enormous responsibility. But then, Nelson was a special leader, in Jake's eyes. He'd distinguished himself from the first moment Jake heard him speak nearly ten years earlier, at a special meeting of the stewards' body, a steamy, closed-door affair convened to allow the big Local's two hundred or so shop stewards to meet privately with the bargaining committee, which had just returned from Toronto split down the middle over a tentative agreement forged only after a four-month strike which had, along with the Americans' war in Vietnam, sent world nickel prices soaring. Half the bargaining committee liked the new agreement, and would recommend acceptance to the full membership, which would hold a ratification vote in a few days' time. But the other half of the bargaining team urged rejection, which meant prolonging the strike into the approaching holiday season. Which way the stewards' body turned would carry considerable weight with the rank-and-file, and might well decide the ultimate outcome. As a result, the meeting, in the Dieppe Room, a much smaller space than the Vimy Room, which was the Hall's main auditorium just across the lobby, was packed with parka-clad stewards shuffling in anxiously in their winter, felt-lined boots. A cloud of cigarette smoke and extreme tension, commingled with the smell of wet wool, hung over the gathering, which was supercharged by a persistent rumour that put the militants on the committee under a cloud of suspicion. Word from Toronto had it that a notorious Detroit-based scrap metal dealer had been seen in the hotel, befriending certain members of the bargaining committee. Ostensibly, the scrap metal man had arrived on a fact-finding mission: would the Sudbury strike continue? The recent dramatic run-up in spot nickel prices had made him a very rich man, scrap nickel being so much in demand by a Pentagon desperate to continue yet another aerial bombing campaign in the skies over North Vietnam. But a return to work in Sudbury would result in an immediate surge of newly finished nickel flooding onto the market, and the bottom would drop out of the scrap price. Never a man to leave matters to chance, the darkest of rumours reaching Sudbury had it that the cigar-chomping Detroiter had been seen whispering confidentially to some bargaining committee members on the elevator, even slipping them bills from the wad of cash he carried in his vest pocket, if only they would prolong the strike ...

Jake was certain that most of the other stewards in the room had heard the same rumours he had, and everyone listened in silence as the bargaining team presented the contents of the tentative agreement, until then a closely guarded secret. The proposed contract was good, if not great—significant wage increases over the life of the three-year agreement, cost-of-living protection against inflation (known as COLA, for short), minor strengthening of contract language—it was clear their strike was beginning to bite. One by one the members of the bargaining committee, arrayed at a table facing the stewards, took turns speaking either for or against the agreement. There was always a heavy element of political posturing at this point, Jake knew. When the bargaining committee faced what was bound to be a raucous membership meeting thronged by a thousand hard rock miners and disgruntled smelter and refinery workers who hadn't seen a paycheck in four months, there was always an irresistible tendency to grandstand, to adopt a militant pose with an eye cocked toward the next election for the local union leadership in the hope that the president who urged acceptance today would be declared a sell-out weakling tomorrow, and who better to replace him than the tough-talking firebrand who had preached rejection, with the promise of "more!" to a membership which seized on the elections as a kind of post facto referendum on the previous contract? If the new contract was good, then the incumbents who had led negotiations stood a good chance of re-election. But if it was found wanting, the incumbent slate would be voted out by an unforgiving rank-and-file. The stakes rose accordingly as a strike dragged on, and by the day of the stewards' meeting it was four-months old, one of the longest strikes in recent memory.

There was a period of silence and the shuffling of feet as the stewards paused to digest the terms of the proposed agreement. Finally someone who Jake, standing at the back of the crowded room, could not see, rose to ask a question. Even craning his neck and standing on his tiptoes the six-foot tall Jake could not quite see the speaker, but his voice carried to the back of the room, loud and clear.

"Well, youse guys have put us in a helluva fix! You want us to do the right thing for the wrong reasons, (Jake surmised he was pointing at the bargaining committee members who were opposed to the contract and wanted to prolong the strike and who were on the take). And you want us to help you sell a goddamned sell-out agreement to the membership! Because that's all this is! And we all know better! We know this strike is just starting to hurt the company! We can't give up now! I say we vote this piece of shit down and send all of youse back to Toronto to get what's been left on the table and to bring back the agreement this membership deserves, goddamnit!"

As the speaker gathered steam Jake could tell the other stewards, listening intently, had swung in support of his impassioned peroration, which was greeted with cheers, whistles, and the stamping of heavy winter boots.

"Who was that?" Jake asked the steward standing beside him.

"Jordan Nelson, Frood Mine," came the reply.

"Huh," Jake nodded. He was impressed, despite Nelson's evidently diminutive stature.

The firebrand Frood Mine steward's argument carried the day in the end, and the stewards' body voted against the contract, which was nevertheless ratified by the full membership by the narrowest of margins. The failure to fully prosecute the strike of '69 was considered the greatest missed opportunity in the history of unionization at Inco, and many a member—and many a steward—vowed never to let the company off the hook so easily ever again.

When the time for Local Union elections rolled around six months after that debacle, Jake was approached by a short, bespectacled figure whom he did not at first recognize. It turned out to be Nelson, who recognized Jake, doubtless because of the exposure he'd received in the fairly recent battle to clean up the Copper Cliff smelter. Nelson was assembling a slate of candidates to run against the old guard currently in power in the Steel Hall. He was pretty sure of his support in the mines, but he was looking to shore up his support in the vote-rich surface plants—there were a thousand votes in the smelter alone, where Jake was well known. Nelson offered Jake a plum spot—Vice President—on the slate, which was heavily weighted with "young guys"—children of the Sixties who tended to be better educated, and a deal scruffier, than the older generation at Inco, many of whom were Second World War vets and "getting up there." Jake asked who else Nelson was considering for his slate before responding to the young miner's offer. Richard d'Aquire's name came up, and that decided the issue for Jake. Once a leader in the smelter cleanup fight, the burly, baldheaded outlaw biker had been fired by the company on a trumped-up charge of threatening a security guard. The union was fighting to have him re-instated, but it was a long, slow process—three stages of grievances before the matter was assigned to an arbitration panel convened by the Ontario Labour Relations Board or OLRB, which had been known to take nearly a year to render its decisions.

"Haywire!" Jake smiled at the memory as he blurted out d'Aquire's nickname. Nelson's choice of d'Aquire for the slate spoke worlds about the young Frood miner. First of all, d'Aquire was still off the job, pending the resolution of his case; his inclusion sent a definite "in your face" message to the company, but to Jake it showed how serious Nelson was—only solid guys need apply. Jake was honoured to be considered for such a group.

"Sure, count me in," Jake told Nelson, and they shook hands, sealing the deal.

Nelson's slate—he'd dubbed his 'Dream Team' the 'Workers' Team'—had come close, but it suffered a narrow defeat to the Old Guard, a group that had a stranglehold on power in the big Local, which was led by literally older men and included Jake's old nemesis Henry Hoople. Hoople had parlayed his position as a shop steward at Garson mine, along with slyly opportunistic support for the Steelworkers in the bitter union infighting of the McCarthy era in the raids against the old Mine Mill, into a slow but steady rise through the union hierarchy.

There were whispers that the election—which was close—had been rigged somehow, rumours that were commonplace in most elections in big, powerful, Steelworker Local Union elections where prize, full-time union jobs were at stake. The victors were rewarded with full-time office jobs that kept them off the job for years, maybe even forever, should they be rewarded with plum, full-time jobs as staff representatives by the United Steelworkers' Pittsburgh head office.

Ballot boxes had a way of disappearing during the crucial over night hours between election day and the actual ballot counting, and there were persistent rumours of irregularities at the polling places, which were located in every mine, mill, smelter division, and refinery across Inco's widely scattered Sudbury operations.

At last, it turned out that there was one honest observer courageous enough to report repeated voting irregularities at the far-flung Levack Mine voting location, and Nelson had seized on the lone whistle-blower's allegations, obtained a sworn affidavit, and parlayed the matter into a full-blown *cause célèbre* within the big International, even carrying his appeal to the giant organization's biannual International Convention in Atlantic City. The Executive Board, anxious to quash even the slightest taint of impropriety at its largest Canadian local, intervened, and ordered a second election in the Sudbury Local, held under strict supervision of the International Union. The result was a narrow victory for Nelson, which sent a tremor through all of Inco's workplaces throughout the sprawling Sudbury operations. Rank-and-file activism surged, and there was, suddenly, a rush of volunteers eager to join the stewards' body in the newly galvanized organization. Resistance to high-handed supervision in all its forms stiffened on the job, and the number of grievances filed soared.

It was as if some huge, terrible, angry beast had just woken up, and Jake and Jordan were riding on the back of the hungry leviathan, hanging on for dear life, lest they be eaten themselves.

At last, Jordan rapped his knuckles on the boardroom table. "All right. It's nine o'clock. Let's get started."

Jake looked around the table, curious to see who else Nelson had invited to the meeting.

"All right," the union president began, gazing at the twenty or so people seated around him, "let's get one thing straight: we're in a war! And you're my War Council, my *consiglieri*."

This was pure Nelson, the reference to the movie *The Godfather*. Jordan always had had a flair for drama. But often, it seemed to Jake, Nelson's apocalyptic premonitions had a way of coming true. It wasn't so much that Nelson was clairvoyant as it was he had some sort of gift of realizing self-fulfilling prophesy, and of making his own gloomy predictions come true. "You're my go-to guys, and I'm gonna be leaning and relying on everybody in this room in the months ahead, is that clear?" A murmur of assent followed, and heads bobbed up and down around the table.

Jake scanned the faces around the room, and found the line-up instructive. Nelson had handpicked only about half the members of the bargaining committee for inclusion in this select group—the ones he trusted, Jake assumed. One face especially stood out: that of Molly Carruth, the only woman at the table. A few years earlier the company had hired a handful of women to serve as production and maintenance employees, Carruth among them. Bright, brassy and quick-witted, Molly had soon become a thorn in the side—for the union, as well as the company—because of her tireless advocacy on behalf of the tiny minority of women in production jobs at Inco, and at the Steelworkers' Hall. For whatever reason, Nelson had taken a shine to her, and now here she was, among the inner circle.

Nelson paused, and glanced down at the handwritten list in front of him. This, too, was a characteristic of the union leader, as Jake would soon come to appreciate: he worried constantly, dwelling on the myriad problems at hand, striving always to stay ahead of the curve, learning to anticipate the next bump in the road.

"I've got this list here, of jobs we're gonna need to get done, and I'm counting on someone from among this group to step up and take them on. First, I need a scrounge, someone who can get us anything we need, and in a hurry, if need be.

"JC, how 'bout you?" Nelson directed the question to Jean Claude Parisé, a little-known but easy-going steward from the smelter, who nodded affably.

"Now this next one is especially tricky: we need someone to take charge of strike pay." It was, they all knew, an especially ticklish issue; even though the amount, twenty-five dollars per week per striker, plus an additional ten per spouse and for each dependent child in the house, was a mere pittance, strike pay occupied a place of great symbolic, psychological, even historic importance, due to the way the old Mine Mill had simply exhausted its treasury back in the strike of '58, and the total amount transferred from Pittsburgh to Sudbury would soon run into millions of dollars.

"And how are we gonna get it to our members?" Nelson concluded. "Brother d'Aquire, are you up for this?"

Jake was taken aback at this selection at first, until he remembered that the outlaw biker held the post of treasurer in the Coffin Wheelers, the local one-percenter's club.

The burly biker nodded his bald head. "Sure. Can do. But who all's getting' paid?" he growled.

Nelson shrugged. "Why not the way we've always done it? By who's on the lines and who isn't?"

There was general assent around the table. Fact was, as they all knew, they might start with eleven thousand-plus members on strike, but that number would soon dwindle as strikers drifted away to take other jobs. Their skills were in wide demand in heavy industry across Canada, after all, and no one begrudged a man who moved away to support his family through what threatened to be a long and nasty winter. This side effect, little understood by outsiders, would hamstring the company over the long haul even more than during the strike itself—many of the decamping strikers would discover greener pastures elsewhere and never return to Sudbury, leaving the company scrambling to fill critical skilled labour shortages in the workplace long after the strike itself had ended.

"Sure," d'Aquire agreed. He turned to face Jake. "But that means you gotta get your captains to take careful attendance." A brief discussion followed as to precisely how many picket line absences would be permitted before strike pay would be disallowed.

Nelson at last cleared his throat, "Speaking of the lines . . ." Here it comes, Jake thought.

"We've gotta get some protocols established on the lines," Nelson insisted.

"Now here's the thing: the company has maintenance it wants to get done while we're out. Re-lining furnaces in the smelter, for one thing, and we've agreed to let those contractors through the lines."

An audible wave of dismay swept across the room. They had just sealed off every mine, mill and refinery behind strong lines, and the picketers would take a dim view of letting anyone through their lines.

"The guys are gonna hate that, Jordan," d'Aquire growled.

Molly Carruth nodded. "It's gonna be hard on the morale out there, and it's sky-high right now, by the way."

Nelson nodded wearily at the dissenting outburst. He knew there was nothing more discouraging on a picket line than opening it up to allow traffic to pass through into a strike-bound plant. Strikers soon began to wonder, sensibly enough, what was the point of their presence. Morale might quickly plummet, and with it, attendance on picket duty. Failure to maintain a strong presence around-the-clock at each of the dozen or so strike-bound operations would be seen as a highly visible sign of flagging support for the strike, a vulnerability the strike leaders could ill afford. Hopefully tying strike pay, measly though it was, to picket duty attendance would help to offset this, but ...

Nelson held up both hands to quiet the dissenting murmur that continued to ripple around the table. "Okay, okay, I get it! But let's be clear about one thing: it's in our own interest to get those furnaces relined."

He thought about the gigantic twin furnaces that were at the heart of the Copper Cliff smelter. Each the size of a high school gymnasium, they were lined with special ceramic bricks, known as refractory brick, capable of absorbing the otherworldly heat required to melt nickel concentrate and turn it into a purer form. The brick was constantly exposed to extreme heat, before being cooled back down. The resulting expansion and contraction of the lining naturally caused the brick to crack and chip and degrade over time, necessitating annual re-lines with new, fresh refractories. It was a spooky, filthy job few of his members wanted, Nelson knew, and for once the union relented in its usual opposition to "contracting out" work on company property to workers who were not Steelworkers. Re-lines also meant furnace shutdowns, resulting in a paucity of work for Local 6500 members in the smelter.

"We've agreed to a protocol for this: nobody in or out unless they're performing routine maintenance in the plants."

"Yeah, and how do we prove they're not going in to start up production?" scowled d'Aquire.

Nelson nodded, as if he'd anticipated just such a question. "We're allowed to stop each vehicle at the lines for three minutes. To talk to the driver, to inspect the vehicle, see what's in it. Three minutes!" He held up three fingers to emphasize his point. "Three minutes. And if our guys see it's copacetic then, and only then, do we wave 'em through." The dissenting buzz around the table subsided to a murmur, before disappearing entirely.

Nelson turned to Carruth. "Molly, I agree morale is a constant worry. I'm glad it's high right now, and we've got to keep it that way. But we've got to explain to our guys out there it's in their interest, too, to let the company get this maintenance done while we're outta the plants, anyways." Nelson held up his hand and wagged a forefinger. "Ain't nobody's doing our guys' jobs here, and that's guaranteed. It's up to us to communicate that to the membership."

But the lone woman at the table frowned. She was stubborn, and militant, Jake reflected, little inclined to bow down to authority, even when that authority was the leader who most all of them loved, and respected.

Sensing her demurral, Nelson hastened on to address another point in his list. "I know by letting the contractors through we risk losing support on the lines. Guys are gonna naturally wonder why they should bust their humps to show up for picket duty if we're just letting vehicles through, anyway. So we need the captains to keep careful attendance records to determine who gets strike pay and who doesn't. Which brings me to another subject: how are we going to actually distribute strike pay? We've got over eleven thousand members out there, scattered from Sturgeon Falls to Espanola. How do we make sure the ones who've earned it get their pay?"

Nelson had a point, and they all knew it. It was an exceedingly complex logistical challenge, given the sprawling nature of the Sudbury Basin. If everyone had to report to the Union Hall for their strike pay they'd have a mob scene.

"De-centralize it." The voice came from somewhere down the table. Jake was surprised to hear it was d'Aquire's.

"Let's organize distribution centres in all the outlying communities. Give me a week to organize a committee. We'll get 'er done."

"All right, Brother d'Aquire, you're in charge of the voucher distribution committee," Nelson readily agreed.

He paused, looking down at the list in front of him. "We've got another problem I wanted to discuss with everyone: prescription drugs. Obviously the company's canceling the drug plan for our members while we're out on strike, even though they still need those drugs. These things are expensive as hell. No way our people can still afford them on strike pay. I was thinking of asking the International Union if Pittsburgh might foot the bill 'til we get back on the job. But this could get tricky, deciding which drugs to cover or not cover, who qualifies and who doesn't, and all that ..."

Finally, Jake raised his hand. "Why not appoint someone from the membership to oversee this? Sounds like it could become a full time job."

Nelson's head bobbed in agreement. "Sure does. And speaking of full-time jobs, we need to get some 'guys' together to form a flying squad to go out on the road and go to plant gates, make speeches, attend rallies, raise money to augment strike pay, keep our name out there ..."

Molly Carruth grinned at Nelson. "Hell, Jordy, why so few guys? We've got over eleven thousand members out there, and not all of them are guys, with all kinds of time on their hands. Why not send anyone who's willing to go?"

Nelson agreed with a weary sigh. "Sure, why not? But it's gonna take a lot of organizing—travel, logistics, booking, that sort of thing—to pull this together, that's all. Sounds like another committee."

"I'll help you find someone."

"Good." Nelson sighed again and checked his watch. "Okay, we need to find someone for the Drug Committee, and a Road Trip Coordinator. That's all I have. Anything else? Anyone? No, well that's it then. Thanks for coming, everyone."

And with that they filed out of the boardroom to face a future that was far more parlous than even the saturnine Nelson had ever imagined.

4

"Every Miner Had a Mother"

Molly Carruth drove straight from the Steel Hall to another meeting—this one of all women—that Jake McCool's wife Jo Ann had called to brainstorm how the women of Sudbury could best support the strike their menfolk were just beginning. Molly supposed she'd been invited due to her high-profile role as an outspoken member of the Local 6500 Women's Committee, but she'd no idea who else had been invited to the meeting at Jake's and Jo Ann's home on Summerhill Crescent, just off Falconbridge Highway, several miles east of the Union Hall.

As usual, the trip out the Kingsway, a dreary, congested four-lane strip of roadway blasted out of solid rock lined with used car lots and fast food joints, was trying to Molly—patience had never been her long suit—but at last she pulled into the short gravel driveway outside Jake's and Jo Ann's home, an unassuming semi-sided in dark brown aluminum, the somber colour being the only feature that distinguished the place in a street full of otherwise identical and nondescript semi-detached duplexes. It wasn't much to look at from the outside, but from the moment she stepped inside the front door Molly was hooked.

Jo Ann Winter-McCool greeted Molly warmly, and the women already present, after joining in on the greeting, returned to their conversation, a buzzing flutter alert to the promise—and the peril—of new times ahead. Molly had never met Jo Ann, a tall, attractive brunette possessed of a pert, lively intelligence that was soon much in evidence as she quietly called the informal gathering to order. Aware that many of her guests had never met, Jo Ann began with a round of introductions, an astute move in Molly's eyes, as it afforded even the most retiring woman in the circle an opportunity to contribute to the discussion.

They were a diverse group that included a professor from Laurentian University, a well-known community organizer, and even Jo Ann's mother-in-law, Alice McCool, who was the matriarch of the group. As they went around the circle and introduced themselves, each woman had been urged by Jo Ann to also explain her interest in building solidarity with the strikers. The university professor expounded briefly on how she'd been drawn to the city to make an academic study of Sudbury's long history in the Canadian labour movement, the community organizer told of the tactics of popular organizing to foster broad public resistance to power in whatever form—she referred in passing to someone named Saul Alinsky—but it was Alice McCool who stole the show that first meeting.

At least a generation older than most of them, she spoke with a quiet authority that was greeted by silent, rapt attention. "I'm here because I've been here once before—in the winter of '58—and that's a place I never, ever want to be at ever again," Alice McCool declared. "It may be the men out there walking that picket line, but don't kid yourselves, it's the women, and especially the wives, who'll make or break this strike!"

She paused to gather her thoughts. Twenty years, almost to the day. And how much had changed! And yet so little. Superficially, at least, the standard of living was now much higher in Sudbury than at the start of the disastrous strike of '58. Everyone had colour televisions, and even two-car families were becoming common. But Alice and her husband Bill saw this new apparent affluence as a house of cards—built on the credit cards that had fueled so much of this abundance. And that was a very real worry now, with this strike upon them. If it wasn't easy credit for consumer goods then it was mortgage-lending policies that encouraged workers to buy ever larger homes and carry ever larger mortgage debt. Thanks to the city's high rate of industrial unionism wages were relatively high—catnip to the big banks and the fly-by-night "finance companies" anxious to induce families to get in over their heads. Late model cars and trucks and larger, glitzier homes were tantalizing, but how tolerant would these lenders be once the steady pay cheques—and the steady payments—stopped? Alice and Bill sensed a terrible vulnerability that might well nip this strike in the bud even before it had truly gained traction. The impulse to live from paycheque-to-paycheque on borrowed money was irresistible. How many of the women in this room hadn't a clue where their next mortgage payment was coming from?

As these thoughts raced through her mind Alice McCool closed her eyes, and memories flashed across her darkened vision. A series of ghostly images—Bill and his brothers Walt and Bud as she'd first met them so many years ago, handsome strong young men, cocky, truculent to a fault, ready to fight at the drop of a hat, their youth tempered now by years spent underground, the fighting spirit they'd channeled into union militancy blunted by the terrible strike of '58 whose loss had ultimately led to the defeat of their beloved Mine Mill; the loss of her son Ben in a bizarre back alley attack which, Alice was still convinced, was somehow political in nature, but a crime that had still never been solved. Ben's death at the hands of an anonymous but lethal attacker in a darkened alley behind the Coulson Hotel had become a deeper mystery, for Alice at least, with every passing year. The tragedy had also embroiled Jake, her youngest boy. He'd been with Ben that night, fighting to protect his brother, but Jake, usually as indomitable with his fists as his father and uncles, had more than met his match at the hands of the mysterious stranger, who put the boots to Ben. Alice had sorrowed deeply for both her sons. Jake, she knew, had blamed himself for Ben's murder—and for a time had withdrawn into some dark place, losing weight, and even his relationship with his girlfriend and high school sweetheart Jo Ann in the process. The swift, at best bittersweet, onrush of memories of her life in this hard rock mining town was nearly vertiginous, and the unexpected jumble of them left Alice almost breathless, and in a swoon. And now here they were, and it was fall, and they were beginning another seemingly hopeless battle against apparently insurmountable odds, and these young, beautiful women, so sweet and fierce in their naiveté were looking up at her for—suddenly Alice McCool, her head beginning to sway alarmingly, came to, opened her eyes, and regained her senses, to the relief of her listeners, who were becoming alarmed at their would-be mentor's insensible silence. Jo Ann was about to scramble to the kitchen to draw her mother-in-law a glass of tap water when she finally came to, and it was true, Alice McCool's mouth was dry, her voice a rasp, when at last she finally spoke a single word.

"Christmas."

"It was Christmas finally broke us. There was no more strike pay, and we'd nothing, nothing don't you see, no turkey dinner, no presents for the kids and we were done, just done for, and the mayor called this meeting of the wives, called us all into the big new arena downtown, and thousands did go, herded in there like cattle ..."

"Did you go, Alice?" queried Jo Ann softly, knowing full well the answer, having heard this story around the McCool supper table at least a thousand times.

"Me? Hell no, I was always a proud member in good standing of the Local 598 Women's Auxiliary and we fought like the dickens against the back-to-work movement—for that's all it was, don't you see? The bosses, the company, oh, they knew all right, how we were suffering for our children, and that was the end of it. The boys went right back to the table, settled for a quickie sell-out agreement which was the very offer the company'd made before we were out for four months—a total defeat—and that was the end. The end of the strike, even the end of the Mine Mill Union, I believe.

"It was Christmas."

A brief silence descended over the room as the women digested Alice's cautionary tale. It was the community organizer who spoke first. "All right, thank you, Mrs. McCool ... Well, I think it's obvious none of us wants to see history repeat itself here, so—any ideas what we should be doing to ensure the same thing doesn't happen to us?"

The university professor was the first to answer. "I think we need to get ourselves organized—mobilize all the wives who support the strike, and support them to support their husbands to keep the strike strong."

Most of the women shared this assessment, as Molly could see.

"Oh, and one other thing," the professor concluded. "We should be especially careful to organize some way to avoid another Christmas let-down ... I know it seems a long way off now, but ..."

"If we even make it that far," one of the younger women reflected soberly.

"Oh, we'll make it," Molly reassured the gathering. "So how about we throw a big Christmas Party for the kids? Every member'd be welcome to bring out all their kids, we'd use the big hall, organize a toy drive first, make a big splash in the media, anybody's thinking of another back-to-work movement because of the holidays we head 'em off at the pass!"

"It could work," the community organizer promptly agreed. "But it's a big job. How we gonna organize this?

I'd be willing to help with this, if anybody else is, but we'd need some standing, some kind of formal recognition, from the union ... Molly, could you help us out with this, act as a go-between for us with the union?"

"A liaison, you mean? Sure, why not? And I'd be happy to let youse know what's happening at meetings, give a woman's point of view ..."

Molly's head was swimming as she made the short drive home from the McCools'. What all had she just agreed to undertake on this first day of the strike? There was finding someone to get the Drug Committee going, she was definitely interested in this new Road Trip Committee, and then everything from the women's meeting—the Christmas Party, playing go-between between the wives and the union. Good thing she was on strike! It was beginning to dawn on her, as it would occur to many, that walking the bricks for a pittance on Pittsburgh strike pay was more work than actually working for wages at Inco. But the time was a gift, and it was about to become the time of her life.

5

Off the Chain

It was baffling, even befuddling, at first: the time.

The sudden sheer enormity of the free time that now loomed before them for—how long?—no one knew. Suddenly the men were home all the time, underfoot now during the day, which strained many marriages, especially if the man was unable or unwilling to share in the housework, and take care of the kids. Many a woman began to nag her husband about this, while in other families the men willingly pitched in with the unfamiliar domestic tasks they had heretofore considered beneath them, and the marriages thrived, and even blossomed.

Many men simply fled to that handiest of male preserves—the garage. At least a large block Chevy V8 358 didn't talk back, and there was a sane, predictable logic to the world of socket wrenches, grease, and WD40.

Still other men found solace in the bush—the vast, mainly trackless Boreal forest that surrounded Sudbury on every side for miles upon empty miles. Some quantum of Indian blood, heretofore ignored, whispered down through the generations and the shiftworker, liberated from the stomach-shredding vagaries of the three-shift schedule, picked up his hunting rifle and repaired to the bush. The snow came early that year, favouring the tracker in pursuit of the biggest game around—moose. A freezer full of moose meat was reproof against the hunger that now lurked at the back of every cabin door, insurance that his family would not go hungry even if they really were "out 'til the grass was green."

Other strikers returned to the trap lines they had inherited from their forebears. Prices for beaver peltries, always cyclical, happened to be especially high that year, one more fallback for the resourceful striker.

Oh, it was a life they loved and had acquired considerable skill at over the years—how to move swiftly and silently over the rugged terrain of the Canadian Shield, how to think like a moose—it would all get easier come freeze-up, when the waterlogged muskeg froze solid, creating a safe, reliable flat path over the boggy swamps that covered every basin and lowland and that were impassable for much of the year. Then, too, the plummeting temperatures would create ideal conditions for ice fishing, with the lakes covered with solid ice several feet deep.

The men of the outlying communities were favoured here—the wilderness was literally in their backyard. Places like Capreol, Levack and St. Charles were located deep in the Northern Ontario bush that was a paradise for anglers and hunters. Americans and outdoorsmen from southern Ontario would drive many miles to reach the abundant, teeming wilderness that was at the strikers' fingertips, and now, for once, there was the time to enjoy it all. Besides, you could eat or sell whatever you shot, caught, snared or trapped. To the resourceful, the strike began as a welcome opportunity to pursue a much-loved, though physically demanding, avocation. The Indian blood whispered, and they were fain to listen.

6

Southern Swing

It came sledding in suddenly, unbelievably early, on an Arctic high-pressure system, and the mercury fell, and kept on falling. The days were noticeably shorter now, and the long dark night of another Northern winter was upon them in earnest.

As it always did, the first true cold snap of winter caught them off guard that year. The sudden surge of savage cold was unbelievable, absolute in its utter indifference, even hostility, to any form of life. How could anyone possibly survive such a thing? And for the many months that stretched endlessly before them now! It hardly seemed possible that only weeks before they'd been "at camp," enjoying languorous long summer days beside cerulean, pure, northern lakes where they'd saunaed before skinny dipping, bodies still steaming, off the end of the dock. Those same lakes were ice-skimmed in the mornings now, and the birch, poplar and cedar that lined the shores gave off loud, sudden reports, like the shot of a high-powered rifle, as the terrible frost entered their bare limbs and trunks, freezing them solid in a trice.

Now, suddenly, the exertion of every living thing was manifest in steamy, billowing exhalations of white clouds that were a stark contrast to the startling deep blue sky. Such clouds puffed out of every head frame, car exhaust, manhole cover and chimney as if in puny earnest that life continued, even in this universe of perishing cold.

At least the first road trip on behalf of the strike was to the south where it was bound to be warmer, Molly reflected as she boarded the rickety old school bus the Local had chartered to transport them to Oshawa and then on to Toronto on a combined fundraising-consciousness raising swing through southern Ontario.

The bus wasn't quite full as it pulled away from the Steel Hall that early morning in November, with thirty or so parka-clad activist members of Local 6500. Molly quickly occupied a window seat so she could enjoy the view as the bus roared south along Highway 69. Jordan Nelson had done the same, but somewhere near Point-Au-Baril the Local Union President was joined by Jake McCool, who slid into the vacant seat beside him.

"Hey, Jake, how's it going?" Nelson greeted his Vice President.

"Not bad, okay, Jordy," Jake replied offhandedly, before lowering his voice. "Can we talk about a few things?"

The union president cast a quick, furtive glance around them before replying in an equally lowered voice. "Sure, Jake, what's on your mind?"

"Well, the women, for one thing ..."

Nelson nodded. "It's tricky, but I think it's a good thing, them getting organized ... I'd a helluva lot rather have 'em inside the tent pissing out, instead of outside pissing in ... Anyway, Carruth is in there, keeping an eye on things ..."

Jake grunted. "I hear that. My wife and mum are both involved, and they're taking it pretty serious ..."

"I know. I heard." Nelson grinned at Jake. "Sounds like you're pretty well surrounded, brother."

Both men fell silent as the bus passed through Point-au-Baril, a strip of non-descript gas stations, hamburger stands, bait shops, and even a one-lung grocery that seemed to double as a liquor store. It wasn't much to look at, but after travelling for an hour-and-a-half through miles and miles of Northern Ontario bush, rivers, lakes, moose pasture, and sheer, steeply-sided rock cuts carved through the Cambrian Shield outcrop that was the understory of all their lives, even this random cluster of buildings was a welcome sight.

At last, Jake resumed his *sotto voce* conversation with Nelson. "So you're thinking of supporting them, then?"

It took the union president an instant to regain the thread of his dialogue with Jake. "Oh. The women, you mean? Hell yeah, I support 'em, but the rest of the Board—I dunno. And that could be a real problem."

Jake nodded. He understood Jordan's worry. Apart from Jake's own vote, the newly elected union president was often outnumbered when it came to crucial matters before the Local Union's full Executive Board, which was comprised mostly of older Steelworker loyalists whose tenure dated back to the days of the Mine Mill-Steel raids. They were by nature a crusty, conservative bunch, suspicious of any new, fresh initiative that lay outside their narrow view of bread-and-butter trade unionism.

"Yeah, well, so far's my mum's concerned it's important. She's anxious to avoid any repeat of '58."

"Sure," Nelson agreed. "But I'm afraid the old guys on the Board will see the exact opposite. They're worried the wives'll get organized and pull a '58 on us all over again."

Jake shook his head in disbelief. "They don't know my mother, then! They have no idea ..."

"No, and do you see anyone budging Carruth over there? Hell, she's more solid than half the guys in this Local—it's some of *them* who worry me the most."

"Oh yeah? How so?"

Nelson shook his head in worry. The President of Local 6500 wore aviator glasses that somehow magnified his eyes and that, so it seemed to Jake, sometimes gave him a mournful, hang-dog look.

"I was on the lines out at Frood, and what I heard out there freaked me right out."

"What happened?"

"Had all kinds of guys, old guys, mainly coming up and telling me it's already a lost cause, that we'll never outlast the company, that we're heading for a repeat of '58 ..." Nelson's voice trailed off.

"Jesus! Where's all that high morale Molly was talking about?"

Nelson gave off a weary sigh. "Beats me. Not on the line at Frood, that's for sure. Some of 'em even wanted me to cancel this trip! Said we're not gonna raise enough money at the gates to even pay for the gas because nobody'll wanna give to support a lost cause ..."

"So what *is* gonna happen on this trip?"

"Jake, I'm honestly not sure. We're going to the plant gates at GM in Oshawa for shift change this afternoon. How that'll go down is anybody's guess. All I know is the Labour Council down there is supposed to have done a little advance work, let 'em know we're coming ..."

Jake nodded and sat in silent reflection as he absorbed Nelson's words. He'd never been to Oshawa, a sizeable industrial city east of Toronto. It was supposedly a labour stronghold where the United Autoworkers Union represented the thousands of assembly line workers who built vehicles for General Motors' Canadian markets, and even shipped cars south, into the U.S. market. But the fact it was a UAW town gave both men pause. Like the Steelworkers, the Autoworkers were organized along industrial lines—they represented all the workers in a given plant or industry, rather than just the workers who specialized in a particular trade or craft— plumbers and pipefitters, stationary engineers, electricians and carpenters. But they were a separate union, and neither Jake nor Jordan actually knew a single member of the big UAW Local at GM personally. How they would be greeted at the plant gates, whether any of the autoworkers even knew, or cared, about the inchoate Sudbury strike was still a complete mystery. How well this thing would go off was dependent on the advance work done by the Oshawa Labour Council where, again, they knew absolutely no one.

All they knew for sure was that Oshawa, and the great, urban megalopolis that sprawled for miles to the west along the shores of Lake Ontario was southern Ontario, a world apart from the smaller, semi-rural outpost towns of the North, which had coalesced around pulp, paper and lumber mills or hard rock mines. It wasn't an altogether different country, but it might have been. The south was more affluent, stable, and settled. Even the landscape was different, with the granitic rock of the Canadian Shield far less in evidence, as was already becoming visible outside the bus windows. The sky was opening up and the terrain flattening as they approached the Severn area, where the Trent Canal spilled into the big water of Lake Huron and Georgian Bay. Now, for the first time, there was a sense they really were leaving the North. The landform here couldn't be described as absolutely flat, but it gave way to gently rolling hills with topsoil evidently deep enough—and rich enough to support agriculture, something rarely seen on the thin, sparse top soils of the North, which often failed to even cover the rocky ribs of the Canadian Shield. The old school bus from Sudbury roared into the rolling hills north of Barrie, toward Toronto, and into the unknown.

It *was* milder, Molly reflected as they trooped off the school bus, but the leaden skies had opened, and it was pouring rain. Like most of her Northern compatriots, Molly had dressed for bitter cold, but moisture? Forget it. Their down-filled outer garments soon lost their loft, and they were all soaked to the skin in minutes by a steady, unrelenting cold rain.

The only bright spot was the greeting that awaited their arrival—a small knot of Oshawa union activists, a mixed group representing the Labour Council and the big UAW Local at GM. They all wanted to meet Jordan Nelson, who was the first one off the bus, Jake marvelled at the change in his friend the moment his boots hit the asphalt of the huge parking lot outside the sprawling GM assembly plant. Gone was the gloomy, introspective Nelson with the weight of the world on his shoulders, replaced instead by a smiling, confident young man, clearly at home with his fellow rank-and-file trade unionists, chatting them up like long lost brothers. Nelson was, suddenly, the centre of attention; he was charismatic in his way, he was their emissary, he was, unmistakably, their leader.

But Molly found herself mesmerized by a tall, trim black man who towered over Nelson. He introduced himself as Wilson Addison, Recording Secretary of the host UAW Local. Addison spoke with a clipped Jamaican accent still redolent of the Islands. "Welcome, welcome brothas and sistas up from Sudbury!" The man was all smiles and dazzling white teeth, but there was, Molly decided, no doubting the sincerity of his welcome. "Now if you will just give me a master copy of your leaflet, suhs, we have our office staff at the ready, Gestetner machines warmed up, at your service to crank out thousands of copies!" Addison eyed Jordan and Jake quizzically, and for the first time

Molly saw Nelson at something of a loss. Truth was, she knew, they had no leaflet—no one had foreseen the need for this simple device to explain their cause to total strangers.

Sensing their embarrassment, Addison cleared his throat and moved smoothly on to the next matter at hand: the exact positioning of everyone outside the plant gate, and not a minute too soon—the very first of the day shift workers coming off shift were beginning to trickle through the gates.

Addison had placed them some distance from the gates, back toward the parking lot, so he could interpose himself between the strikers and the gate. As soon as the workers began to spill from the gates, he began his stream of constant, non-stop chatter. "Okay, now ma brothas we got folks down from Sudbury ovah there, be needin' our support! They're in vera deep, out on strike against them mean mothafuckas at Inco, which be one evil, mean and nasty Yankee-owned mining company puttin' it to our Canadian brothas and sistas from up in there! So dig deep, brothas, dig deep, and show them the kinds of men we got here in Local 222! Remember, an injury to one is an injury to all! So dig deep, ma brothas, dig deep!"

Molly found herself smiling at Addison's non-stop verbal barrage despite the trickle of cold rainwater that was just beginning to run down her back. But their host's boundless enthusiasm for the cause was infectious, and, sure enough, each autoworker emerging through the plant gate straightened up, squared his shoulders, and began digging into the pockets of his blue jeans. Soon enough the metallic sound of coins hitting the bottoms of their buckets became a steady, almost symphonic rhythm. "Thanks, brother, thank you, thank you." Jake, Jordan and Molly began to mutter.

Everything had just settled into a quiet, smooth routine when it happened. An autoworker had just flipped a coin into Molly's bucket when she felt him reach out and squeeze her left breast! It wasn't a gentle fondle, either. Molly reacted, instinctively, as any industrial strength Sudbury union maid would have: with a swift, vicious, unerring kick to his groin. She hadn't worn her steel metatarsal guard that day, but she had worn her steel-toed work boots, which found their mark in a flash. She didn't drop the guy, but he did make a funny face, and a funny sound, "Ooooh! Ooooh!" as if he were having trouble breathing. Well, good! Molly was heartily sick of this shit! The harassment on the job at Inco was nearly as bad from the guys on the job, she'd discovered, as it was from the company. No one had really wanted women in hourly-rated jobs at Inco, as they daily reminded Molly and the handful of women who'd been hired with her. She was no bra-burner—not one of your women's libbers—but she was by God, just as entitled to a decent-paying job to support her family—as much as any man. As it seemed to have a way of doing, commotion and consternation swirled around the quick-witted, sharp-tongued Molly Carruth, and now it had followed her even here, to the plant gates outside a beJeezus big automobile assembly plant in Oshawa, Ontario.

Jordan Nelson had had his back turned at the moment of the boob grab and the swift retribution that followed, but he sensed there was trouble and quickly whirled around to confront Molly. He eyed the autoworker who was still clutching his privates, still struggling to inhale, not moaning exactly, but still only able to muster a low, mewling almost bird-like sound, "Oooooh, Ooooh."

"Jesus, Carruth!" Jordan rounded on Molly. "What did you just do?"

"He grabbed my boob, Jordy! Swear to God he did!"

Nelson surveyed the scene once again, and did a quick mental calculation: yes, it was true they were down here as honoured guests—mendicants, really—and Carruth had put the entire unfamiliar and not quite comfortable situation at risk. But as he looked into her angry brown eyes, pleading with him, almost beseeching his understanding, his anger melted away. A Toronto TV news team, led by reporter David Goldstein, was on the scene, but the cameraman had just then been changing film magazines and so missed the shot of a lady Sudbury Steelworker's swift kick to the groin of an Oshawa Autoworker, much to Goldstein's displeasure. Whatever had happened, it had not been captured on film, to be aired over and over again. Luck was with them, but only just. "Okay, Molly, okay. You did the right thing, then." Nelson placed a reassuring hand on Carruth's shoulder.

Order had just been restored and the sound of coins hitting bucket bottoms resumed when "Haywire" d'Aquire approached and tapped Nelson on the shoulder.

57

"Hey Jordy, got a minute? There's somethin' over here I think you should see."

The union leader turned and dutifully followed d'Aquire to the spot, just a few paces away, where his crew was conducting their own collection. D'Aquire pointed at their bucket. "Check it out."

Nelson peered into the bucket, and was amazed to discover it was half full, not only of coins, but also of bills—one's and two's mainly but, even a few five's, ten's, and twenties.

Nelson was stunned at the sight, but also bemused—suddenly, his recent worries about even covering the cost of diesel for this trip seemed ludicrous.

Haywire gestured toward other knots of Sudbury Steelworkers who were further down the line, each group with its own bucket. "Same thing all the way to the parking lot, boss."

For the union president, the implications of all this were huge—too huge to grasp. His immediate concern must be his troops around him, and they were all cold and wet. He reached into his pants pocket, pulled out his wallet, extracted a credit card, and handed it to d'Aquire. He spoke softly. "Okay, brother, here's what I want you to do: I'll get someone from 222 to drive you over to their hall, use their phones to book us into the best motel in town, and we'll all take the bus there, have a hot shower and clean up before we head into Toronto, yes? We'll settle up when we get home."

"You got it, brother," d'Aquire assured him.

And with that, Nelson turned to go back up the line, to locate Wilson Addison, to inform him of the wondrous thing that had just transpired, and to thank him, with all the humble gratitude of a drowning man who has just been rescued from near-certain death.

As per Nelson's wishes, the whole crew were soon ensconced, however briefly, in Oshawa's best motel.

Amid a general rush for the showers, there was also an attempt by a few Frood miners—who will remain nameless—to short circuit the cable television connection at the back of the in-room television sets in an attempt to obtain free cable. Many wanted to see the hockey games, but the porn channels were also of special interest. In the event, little came of this attempted petty larceny, much to the disappointment of the delegation from Sudbury, where cable television remained a rare, and expensive, novelty.

With a weary sigh, Jordan Nelson herded his unruly charges back on the bus. After a hasty head count he nodded to the driver.

Next stop: Queen's Park in downtown Toronto, where, it was hoped, the Sudbury strikers could drum up some interest in their cause among the dozens of reporters in the Queen's Park press gallery.

The union president heaved a sigh of relief when, head count completed, the school bus began to lumber its way toward the 401. The unpredictable chaos of a mass plant gate fundraising lay behind them. Ahead lay the august, orderly precincts of Ontario's legislative assembly, Nelson reassured himself.

What could possibly go wrong?

Even after their showers and hasty clean-up, the Sudbury strikers, in their still half-damp union parkas and shaggy haircuts and beards, were still a motley crew to behold as they were issued into the visitors' gallery overlooking the floor of the Legislature, just then in session.

By pure coincidence, the MPP for Sudbury, Harry Wardell, was just wrapping up a rather long-winded question to the Tory party then in government.

It may also have been coincidence that the visitors' gallery had steeply banked seats that looked directly down on the government benches far below. Graying hair, receding hairlines, and altogether bald pates were much in evidence to the group. The difference in age and attire—sombre pin-striped three-piece business suits seemed much in vogue among the Tory ranks, and there were at least two generations' difference in age—was striking.

Wardell's question concerned the strikers themselves, whom he welcomed as they were being ushered in to the stately chamber. The group had been sternly warned that any sort of demonstration in the grand, historic, chamber was strictly forbidden, would be ruled indecorous, and would result in their immediate expulsion by the hefty security guards hovering suspiciously nearby.

The bus that had brought them down from Sudbury made a single stop between Oshawa and Queen's Park, at the Steelworker's Toronto headquarters on Cecil Street, where the union's professional communications experts had similarly counseled against any sort of overt demonstration. Instead, they had

demonstrated their newly hatched fundraising stratagem, tin cans with slots cut in the top, in the manner
of a piggy bank. Wrapped around the cans was a
brightly coloured paper wrapper urging "Nickels for
the Nickel Strikers." Best to prime the pump, the
Steelworkers' professional comms people had advised,
by dropping a few coins—five pennies, say—into the
can and rattling them around to attract the attention
of would-be donors. The group was present only to
draw attention to the Sudbury strike in the most
orderly and seemly manner, armed only with a visual
prop—the tin cans with slots cut in the top, labeled
"Nickels for etc. etc."

But the Sudbury delegation, in its perch high
above the government benches, soon grew restive
as the speeches below them droned on and endlessly
on. They were, after all, a roistering rough-and-
tumble lot, used to stoking blast furnaces or blast-
ing muck out of solid rock. Unaccustomed to sitting
idle for extended periods in the middle of a workday,
they soon began to fidget like small children in
church.

Molly herself felt this unease, sitting doing nothing with this stupid can in her hand, when she first
began to hear it—the steady plink-plink-plink of
small change hitting the bottom of a can. Evidently
one of her compatriots had decided to take advantage
of this break in the action to charge his can in the
manner suggested by the union's PR people. The
sound itself was really quite muted, but it started a
trend, not unlike the first few fat raindrops falling
onto the surface of a placid northern lake. Molly

could sense she was not alone in hearing the steady, mischievous insinuation of the pennies hitting the bottom of the can. Soon enough she could see other strikers wiggling in their seats, digging in their pants pockets for loose change. In seconds the plunk-plunk-plunk of pennies could be heard throughout the visitor's gallery, the first few warning drops now quickly become a bursting torrent. Once the cans were charged there was nothing for it but to test them by shaking them in the air. And sure enough, the pennies rattling around inside made a fine racket—the more so when amplified by thirty or so Sudbury strikers. The metallic rattle soon drowned out whichever MPP was unlucky enough to have the floor and Molly was treated to the unforgettable sight of the alarmed looks of the aged Tories below, all bedecked in their finest legislative finery, looking up at the visitor's gallery with expressions of commingled annoyance and alarm. What a shambling rabble! The barbarians were no longer at the gates, but were now clearly well inside of it.

"Order! Order! This House will come to order!" barked the Speaker of the House, ensconced in his red plush awe-inspiring throne.

Molly watched the reaction on the floor, where she noticed Harry Wardell laughing as he looked up at them, evidently enjoying the chaotic spectacle immensely.

"Order! Order! This House will come to Order at once!" bellowed the Speaker, red-faced now as he rose to his feet. The pages who encircled the Speaker's imposing Chair on its elevated dais, high school honours students all, attired in matching white shirts and black pants, all snapped smartly to attention as the Speaker rose.

"Adjourned!" yelled out the Speaker. "I now declare this session adjourned! Sergeant-at-Arms will you now clear the House, and especially the Visitor's Gallery!"

And with that the Security Guard began to shoulder his way brusquely amidst the Steelworkers, until one of them blocked his way. It was Eldon Critch. A lifetime spent in Frood Mine had done nothing to diminish his stature, and he stood a head taller than the blonde-haired, blue-eyed security guard who was his junior by several decades. "Don't put your hands on me," Critch warned the younger man in a steady, even tone. "I fought my way through every major battle in the Second World War and if you don't stand aside, laddy buck, I assure you I will personally insert that fine starched uniform into a place where it will require dry-cleaning before you can wear it again." The younger man stepped meekly aside as the Steelworkers filed out of the Visitors' Gallery of their own accord.

The scene was nowhere near as orderly in the Press Gallery at the end of the legislative chamber where everyone, it seemed, had begun a simultaneous stampede for the exits. After sitting in stunned, suspended animation as the spectacle before them unfolded, the reporters had suddenly, and simultaneously, been struck by the epiphany that they were witnessing history—never before had the Ontario Legislature been forced to adjourn by an unruly outburst within its precincts. There's nothing an editor appreciates more than a legitimate, bona fide superlative, and so each of them bolted at once for the doors, eager to "scoop" all the others.

"Well, Jordy, I think the world knows there's a strike on in Sudbury now," Jake smiled wryly at Nelson as the bus headed north up Avenue Road.

It was at least Honey Harbour before the buzz had begun to die down, and Jake was able to slide into the vacant seat beside Jordan Nelson once again. "Jordy, I've been thinking …"

"Oh yeah? 'Bout what?"

"What that black guy from 222 said back there on the line … I think he was right—we do need some kind of leaflet explaining what the strike is all about."

"Okay, Jake, but there's just one problem—I ain't no writer and neither are you. So who we gonna get to write this thing?"

"Well, that's just it. I know this guy …"

7

Mission to Bay Street

Was there any place on Earth, Harry Wardell wondered, he hated more than Bay Street, the downtown Toronto epicenter of Canadian capitalism?

The proud towers of Canada's Big Six chartered banks, phallic tributes to the men who ruled the country, crowded the sky, each tower taller than the last, as if in some colossal dick-swinging contest.

But, like it or not, he was in for it now, Wardell had to admit as he entered the Wellington Street entrance to CIBC Plaza. The acronym, fittingly, stood for "The Canadian Imperial Bank of Commerce." Imperial, indeed! The member of the provincial legislature from Sudbury spared a scowl for the security guard sitting behind his desk at the bank entryway. The guard himself reciprocated with a suspicious nod at the gangly figure who strode past him with his curious, head-first gait.

Wardell bit back the revulsion he felt at his surroundings—he had a job to do here. It was the day after the Sudbury strikers had shut down the Legislature by creating an uproar in the visitors' gallery, and Wardell was here in this place he hated—on their behalf. The strike was now well into its second month, and that meant thousands of Harry's constituents had now missed two consecutive mortgage payments. He and his two fellow party members from Sudbury's three provincial seats had divvied up the six big banks who held the paper among themselves, and Harry had drawn the Royal and the Imperial, and now here he was, about to keep an appointment with the CEO of the Imperial Bank himself. The purpose of their respective missions to Bay Street was to expend what little political capital they might have with the Lords of Bay Street to "jawbone" the bankers into relenting on any planned foreclosures against any strikers in the Sudbury area, unpaid mortgages notwithstanding.

Harry didn't much like his chances as he boarded the elevator and pushed button number "73." His meeting was with CIBC CEO Clarence McCaskill, who also sat on Inco's Board of Directors. Fat chance he'd agree to any measure that appeared to favour the strikers' side in the Sudbury dispute. But Wardell and his two legislative cohorts had anticipated this obvious challenge and, in private consults with strike leader Jordan Nelson they had quietly devised a plan ...

The crowd in the elevator car, which had been packed in on the ground floor, had thinned out quite noticeably as the elegant vehicle—even its walls appeared to be marble—continued its speedy, ear-popping ascent.

At last it braked smoothly to a halt, the double doors slid open, and Wardell stepped into a room of quiet, understated elegance where all sound, including the steady electronic pulsing of telephones, was muted. The lighting was indirect, the carpet was plush, and the walls were lined with large, to Wardell's eye abstruse, but doubtless very expensive, works of abstract art. He strode toward the receptionist's desk, which faced the elevator. It was staffed by a very pretty young woman, who eyed Wardell's rumpled three-piece corduroy suit with the dubious look of a Holt-Renfrew veteran.

"Looking for Clarence McCaskill."

"Do you have an appointment, sir?"

Wardell nodded. "Yes, for ten-thirty. I'm a bit early."

She summoned an icy smile. "I see. Mr. McCaskill is in conference just now. Won't you take a seat?" She waved him toward a seating area adjacent to her curved desk.

Wardell dutifully took a seat on one of the couches arranged around a glass coffee table scattered with glossy magazines.

The Sudbury MPP idly surveyed the covers of the magazines—*Fortune, Business Week,* and *Canadian Business.* About what he'd expected to find. Reading material designed to reinforce the Cult of the business leader as wise and worthy steward of the Canadian economy. A quote from that savvy old hippy Stewart Brand entered Wardell's mind: "Beware, beware controlling all your own inputs lest you become a caricature of yourself."

"Mr. McCaskill will see you now." Her tone was somewhere between icy and welcoming. Not worth dwelling on, Wardell decided, as he stood up and moved toward the solid wood door that she gestured to. Without being fully conscious of it, Wardell took a deep breath, like a man about to enter battle.

Which is exactly what he was.

It was a corner office, naturally, and McCaskill was overshadowed by the spectacular view of the Toronto skyline and Lake Ontario framed by the floor-to-ceiling windows at his back. The banker did not rise to greet Wardell, but remained motionless behind his desk. "Mr. Wardell... please, do sit down." He motioned at a chair facing his desk, and the stunning view.

"Now, to what do I owe the, um, pleasure of your visit?"

"I was hoping to speak to you about the strike in Sudbury, or rather the fallout from it."

McCaskill frowned. "I see. I am aware of the dispute of which you speak, of course, but as a member of that corporation's Board of Directors I'm afraid there's really nothing I can say or do—"

Wardell cut him off with a sudden, dismissive wave of his hand. "I'm interested in your role here, sir ... "

"And what concern is that of the Canadian Imperial Bank's?"

"Mortgages, Mr. McCaskill, mortgages. You hold the paper on the homes of hundreds, if not thousands, of Sudbury Steelworkers, and it's come to our attention that your bank is considering foreclosure actions against them."

McCaskill nodded. "That may well be, but only if they have failed to make two consecutive monthly payments will they receive written notice of our intention to initiate foreclosure proceedings."

"We'd like your assurance, sir, that no such actions will take place ..."

"Whaaat? We have an agreement with those people, sir, and foreclosure is our legal right in the event an account goes into arrears."

Wardell knew, as his adversary must have, that wholesale foreclosures would have a devastating impact on the Sudbury housing market. The eviction of thousands of families, with as many houses standing vacant and suddenly put up for sale, would collapse prices for all residential property, whether the mortgage was in arrears or not. Sudbury was a city of homeowners, and their equity would be wiped out overnight. Not on my watch, Wardell thought grimly.

"You have how many branches in Sudbury, sir?"

McCaskill appeared caught off guard at the apparent non sequiter. "What? Oh, I really couldn't say offhand ... Perhaps a dozen, I suppose."

Wardell nodded. "A dozen banks ... Twelve thousand strikers, plus twelve thousand wives. That makes twenty four thousand. Let's assume two kids per family, that's forty eight thousand. What's that add up to, Clarence?" Wardell unfolded his long frame from the chair and leaned forward for emphasis. As always, the gesture, plus the look of pure menace on his face, had the effect of a venomous snake coiling, readying for a strike. "Because that's how many new savings accounts those branches will have next Monday when each of those union families, and their kids, open savings accounts to deposit their strike pay and then immediately decide to withdraw it, a dollar at a time.

"I've never seen a run on a bank, but I've heard what one looks like—long lineups at the wickets, pushing and shoving begins, panic sets in ...

"And I foresee very long lineups in Sudbury, sir— never ending, in fact. I know I'd be panicked, if I were a legitimate bank depositor, a small business person seeking a loan, or whatever."

"The whole thing would look like a train wreck, and who knows the national fallout once the story reached the national nightly TV news?"

McCaskill listened as if thunderstruck. His expression darkened from gloom to an outright scowl. "But these individuals are adults, sir. They took certain responsibilities upon themselves when they elected to embark on this, this, adventure when they voted to reject a perfectly good offer from the company and follow this Pied Piper of a leader they have up there— what's his name? Judson? Nelson?"

"Nelson. Jordan Nelson."

"But this is all madness, pure madness, even you must see that—what did your own leader—and I'm no great fan of his, or of your party, as you may well imagine—even he called these strikers 'The Archie Bunkers of the Left.'"

It was all Wardell could do to suppress a wince as the banker's words struck home. It was true that his own party leader had used precisely that memorable turn of phrase to describe the Sudbury strikers. The reference to a redneck working class character on a popular American television sitcom had made for great, crowing headlines in the big Toronto dailies, even as they outraged Jordan Nelson. The youthful union leader had vented that outrage on Wardell and his colleagues during their private meeting following the strikers' disruption of the House. All three Sudbury MPPs were mortified at their leader's remarks, and they quietly seethed as Nelson berated them. Meetings like this one with McCaskill helped re-direct much of that anger.

But Wardell managed to maintain his poker face, and he merely shrugged at the banker's remarks.

"No one's proposing anything illegal here, sir, or violent. But the optics of long line-ups at the tellers' windows, well, these people have nothing better to do—eleven thousand pissed off hard rock miners with nothing but time on their hands ..." Wardell's voice trailed off. " ... there's just no telling how this thing could end ..."

"So what you're asking is ...?"

"That you halt any and all foreclosure actions immediately, and for the duration. We'll call it a draw. You cease and desist, and so do we ... This meeting never happened, and nor did the ones my Sudbury colleagues are about to have with the other five big chartered banks here on the Street. Your Sudbury branches are off limits to strikers and their families, and their homes are off limits to the bailiffs. You send out notices to your Sudbury branch managers that they are to take no actions against mortgagees in arrears during this strike, we shake hands on it, I leave this place, we never see each other again, and no one knows this meeting ever happened."

With that Wardell unfurled his lanky frame, stood up, smiled for the first time that morning, and reached across McCaskill's desk to shake hands with the banker, and that is where matters have stood.

Until now.

8

Molly Keeps the Peace

"No! I don't want it! Who let you in here? You shouldn't be in here! We don't want your kind anywhere near this union hall!"

Molly Carruth could hear the angry male voice, quivering with emotion, even before she'd reached the foyer doors to the Vimy Room. The speaker was Eldon Critch, with whom she'd just made the Toronto trip. She knew him as a well-respected Frood miner, a Second World War combat veteran, and loyal Mine Miller, proud even in defeat. He was berating one of the Wives, Brenda Joyce, a shy, petite redhead, who was trying to pass him a leaflet about the impending Christmas Party. The veteran miner towered over the much smaller Joyce, who was standing her ground nonetheless.

Carruth hurried over to the unlikely combatants. "Whoa! Whoa!" she yelled, to draw their attention. "What's going on here, Brother Critch?"

"She shouldn't be in here!" Critch responded, pointing down at Brenda Joyce. "This isn't 1958 and we want no part of any Wives' movement to get us back to work ..." the older man sputtered.

"Whoa, whoa, settle down there Eldon!" Molly responded immediately. "It's a Christmas Party!" That's all it is, a Christmas Party! It's not about breaking the strike! It's about making sure we don't make the same mistake as in '58! This is Wives Supporting the Strike, Eldon! I'm in this organization, too! You know me! Do you think I'd be part of any sort of back-to-work movement? C'mon, Eldon!"

The burly Frood miner began to simmer down, and he appraised the women anew, tilting his head just so to see them better through his bifocals. Behind the hostile glare, Molly could see, were blue eyes that were not unfriendly.

In one action-packed week since their return from the Toronto trip, the strike had begun to take shape in earnest through a variety of measures:

- The Local Union Executive had voted to formally recognize the Wives Supporting the Strike group as friendlies, and authorized them to use Union premises for their activities. The vote had carried by the narrowest of margins only after Jordan Nelson, at Molly's urging, had staked his own personal credibility on the women's group.
- The Wives had buckled down and begun concerted efforts toward a seemingly impossible goal: a Christmas party for all the union children affected by the strike, lacking only presents for fourteen thousand or so children.

And so Molly explained to the agitated Eldon Critch, whose blue eyes began to soften behind his bifocals as he stared down at the diminutive, but determined, women before him.

Even an agitated, suspicious old Mine Miller had to admit what Molly Carruth—who was a fellow union member, after all—was saying made sense.

9

Below the Water Line

Even as turmoil and controversy roiled the restive waters of the Union Hall that fall, below the water line, far to the south, the big Local's bargaining committee lay becalmed and in the doldrums. Morale among the committee's members was at an all-time low, and that worried Jordan Nelson. As Christmas approached, the Royal York Hotel, the luxurious downtown Toronto hotel that was traditionally the site of Inco-Union bargaining, was increasingly decked out in Christmas décor, which only accentuated the homesickness felt by the Sudbury trade unionists. The Royal York, a huge 1930s-era hostelry that had hosted English royalty, and a constellation of Hollywood and Broadway A-list guests in its forty year history, had begun to feel more like a maximum security prison than a five star hotel to Nelson's crew. Some guys were drinking more than usual, and personal enmities were beginning to flare, a fatal flaw the company would surely seek to exploit at the bargaining table. Already the company's bargaining team had taken not-so-subtle pokes at Nelson personally, pointing out that he was single, without children awaiting Santa Claus.

Nelson was unsure what effect this divisive tactic was having on his team, but he couldn't help taking it to heart. It was true—he was the only single guy on the committee, the only one without a family. In that sense he was an outlier—not just here in Toronto among the bargaining committee, but in Sudbury, also, among the eleven thousand-strong rank-and-file army he was leading. Sudbury was very much a family-oriented place, where successive generations had laboured in the mines, mills, and smelter. Family roots ran deep up there, save for Jordan Nelson himself, who was a first generation Sudburian, living alone, single and childless.

Team morale also wasn't helped by the state of play of bargaining that Christmas season, for the fact was there was no bargaining. Oh, the provincial government had appointed a crack team of its best labour mediators in an effort to kick-start negotiations, but to date, and with Christmas fast approaching, their efforts had proved unavailing.

Jordan met often with the mediators, who shuttled constantly back and forth between the dueling bargaining committees in a ceaseless search for even the thinnest sliver of common ground upon which they could base a resumption of face-to-face talks, but even the faintest glimmer of hope for such an outcome was lacking, and so whole weeks had passed—soon becoming months—without the resumption of full-on collective bargaining. The stalemate—and the enforced idleness and boredom that were eating away at Jordan's bargaining team—was only reinforced by the bright holiday gaiety that pervaded the grand old hotel facing Union Station on Front Street. Long a social hub of Toronto's business elite, the Royal York was a constant swirl of Christmas gatherings, office parties, and sundry seasonal events that only served to underscore how far the Sudbury workers were from home and their own loved ones. Although it was a huge place, even the Royal York was soon bulging at the seams from the press of the season's myriad social demands, and this, too, became a problem. Every nook and cranny of the Royal York was booked solid for some kind of holiday gala, family gathering, dance or concert. Even if they could pull a genuine bargaining session together, the mediators soon discovered, there was no room at the inn. Every one of the hotel's twelve hundred-plus rooms was full—except for one.

They met but once—and that only for a few hours—a few days before Christmas Eve, and the moment was unforgettably surreal. The venue was the Ball Room of the Royal York Hotel. It was a last-ditch, Hail Mary attempt by the mediators to gauge whether the season might have softened attitudes on either side.

There they were, seated facing one another at parallel tables in the middle of the parquet wooden dance floor of the gilt-encrusted grand old room, dwarfed by their surroundings, the impossibly high ceilings and garish crystal chandeliers. It was like a scene right out of the Cold War, two adversaries facing off, each capable of ending the world, or an entire city, with thousands of lives hanging in the balance

The union side faced a problem the company did not—no one was quite sure what was happening on the ground, in real time, back home in Sudbury. Every member of the committee had a source—usually a wife—but their reports varied widely in a fashion that confounded them all. This one had a wife in Levack, a satellite mining town on the furthest fringes of the Sudbury district, who reported an entire community in malaise, depressed by the harshness of the winter, the absence of work, and the growing scarcity of money, while the guy next to him, who hailed from the old smelter town of Coniston, which was much closer to downtown Sudbury than far-flung Levack, received word that the privation engendered by the strike was making the community more tightly-knit, that resolve was growing, and that morale was high. Were both accounts accurate, or neither? Given the distance between the two towns it was entirely possible both reports were true, but who really knew? They were like the proverbial circle of a dozen blind men trying to describe an elephant entirely by feel.

In this, at least, the company had an advantage. Its informational supply lines were much shorter and more compact. Front line supervisors remained on the job, reporting to their superiors, who passed word up the chain of command to Mahogany Row in Copper Cliff, and thence down to world headquarters in Toronto. Where the company was at a distinct disadvantage was in accurately gauging the mood among the rank-and-file.

In the event the mediators' efforts came to naught that bizarre day just seventy-two hours before Christmas Eve. Neither side was willing to present a new offer, and the session ended abruptly, and coldly. It was now clear both sides were digging in for the winter.

The union negotiators packed their bags, surrendered their room keys, and set out, still empty-handed, for Sudbury, unsure of what greeting awaited them.

10

The Kindness of Strangers (1)

Being in Sudbury, they soon discovered, was like being in a different world. The snow-covered city, though bitterly cold, seemed in a state of freeze-dried suspended animation, apprehensively awaiting the outcome of the only thing that mattered: the strike itself.

The bargaining committee members, and especially Jordan as its leader, were immediately besieged by the Sudbury news media: how were the talks going? Had there been any progress at the bargaining table? What was the outlook? And, above all, was there any end to the strike in sight? Nelson and his colleagues did their best to fend off the persistent horde with vanilla, non-committal answers that concealed the grim reality that there were no talks, there was no progress at the bargaining table, and even less prospect for an end to the strike any time soon, and Merry Christmas to you, sir. They were careful not to raise false hopes without at the same time dashing too many, either. It was a delicate, exhausting balance that drove home a major advantage to bargaining in Toronto; the media scrutiny was much more desultory down there, at least a partial offset to the isolation and homesickness they all felt, lost in the bowels of the big city.

The buzz around the Union Hall was all about the Wives' impending Christmas Party. Here, too, there was apprehension: while notice of the affair had gone out to the local news media, there was still considerable doubt that the Wives could pull off a successful event.

Presents remained a problem. While Jordan had ordered the newly formed Scrounge Committee to put on a full court press soliciting the donation of kids' presents from local merchants, the results had been mixed at best. With the countdown on and the date for the Party fast approaching, the Scroungers' meager haul lay in a small pile in a corner of the Vimy Room for all to see.

"That's it?" Nelson turned to Carruth. It was evening of yet another bone-chilling day, with wind chills approaching thirty below, and the Hall was deserted. Their words echoed off the ceiling and walls of the cavernous room.

"Yeah, that's all there is," Carruth agreed with a reluctant sigh.

No one knew what a pile of Christmas presents for fourteen thousand kids looked like, exactly—who had ever even dreamed of such an audacious event?—but clearly this wasn't it.

Jordan shook his head. "We're not even close. Should we cancel?"

Carruth answered with a shake of her own head, refusing to admit the Wives had been beaten. "Naaah,

Jordy, we can't cancel. There's still a few days yet …
Let's just wait and see what happens and hope for the
best …"

The strike leader, weary to the bone at the great
press of responsibility that had been foisted upon
him, already sick to death—as they all were—at the
severity of a winter that had only just begun, relented
with a sigh. "All right, Carruth, but Jesus I hope you're
right about this …"

With the news media already invited to attend the
Wives' Party, they were well and truly backed into a
corner. But the fact was, there was some hope that
someone, somewhere would hear their prayer and
that some last minute help might arrive. Even before
they'd left Toronto Jordan had been busy, travelling
incessantly, appearing as a featured guest speaker at
rally after rally organized by individual local unions
and Labour Councils, first around the province, and
then, increasingly, all over the country as word of the
titanic struggle unfolding in Sudbury began to
spread. The can demo inside Queen's Park had generated bemused but sensational headlines all across the
country, and it soon became apparent that the touch-
ing rank-and-file generosity the Sudbury strikers had
experienced at the Oshawa plant gates was not an
isolated aberration. Wherever he went, Jordan was
showered with cheques and cash donations from
fellow unionists, and the numbers had started to add
up. And the "Nickels for Nickel Strikers" cans were
beginning to come in, too, just as the Steelworkers'
Toronto communications people had foreseen,
jammed with coins, yes, but often stuffed with bills.

Some Steel locals, like 1005, which represented the thousands of workers at the giant Hilton Works of the Steel Company of Canada in Hamilton, had placed a can on every table of the union hall taproom, while other, smaller union locals—many of them not even Steelworkers—had placed the cans in workplace cafeteria lunchrooms on company property. Often this gesture was met by hostility and threats from the employer, which the union in question then resisted, and in this way the militant mobilization by Sudbury's workforce began to have repercussions far beyond Inco's own strikebound plants. The Sudbury struggle was a germ, and it was spreading.

That word of Sudbury's travails had travelled all the way to Canada's West Coast became apparent to Jordan Nelson when he accepted an invitation from the B.C. United Fishermen and Allied Workers Union in Vancouver to give a speech there. The Sudbury union president was moved at the warmth of his reception, due, at least in part, to the respect the Sudbury Union had always accorded the militant Fishermen's Union in its own battles with B.C. fish plant owners. Dating back even to the days of the old Mine Mill, Sudbury unionists had been renowned for their generosity in supporting striking trade unionists across the length and breadth of Canada. Now it was time to repay the favour.

"Would you guys like some fish?"

The question from the President of the B.C. Fishermen's Union took Nelson aback. "What? Oh, sure, no doubt our members would like that," Jordan Nelson nodded appreciatively.

"We'll ship some back East to you, then. Try to get 'em there before Christmas," the UFAWU President vowed.

"You Jordan Nelson, President of this here outfit?" Judging by the company logo sewn into his work shirt, the questioner was a driver for a courier company—hardly an unusual occurrence at the Steel Hall as Christmas approached. Random, unexpected deliveries of goods were pouring in now—everything from foodstuffs to children's Christmas toys—as if the season of good will had opened some kind of flood gates, and thoughts and well wishes were now turned to the strikebound Nickel City, lying inert and exposed to the winter's terrible cold.

"Yeah, that's me," Nelson confirmed.

"Okay then. Sign here." The courier proffered a bill of lading for the union president's signature.

"Whad'ya bring me?" Nelson inquired with scant real interest.

"Fish," came the reply. "Lots of 'em. 'Bout ten thousand pounds of frozen fish."

"Yeah? No shit." Nelson had all but forgotten the B.C. Fishermen's Union President's promise of a present of fish, what with all the pre-Christmas bustle and excitement around the union hall. It was after hours, and he'd repaired to his office to share a joint with Jake and Molly, two members of his inner circle with whom he felt the closest.

"Let's go have a look," Nelson suggested to his companions, and they all trooped out of Nelson's second floor office.

"It's a reefer, so I'll just leave it parked out back," the courier explained as they trudged downstairs to the door to the back parking lot. "Instructions say it's s'posed to be left running at all times."

"Yeah?" Nelson was incredulous. "Jesus, in this cold it's not like any cargo inside's gonna thaw out!"

At last the little group arrived at the back end of a five-ton cube van, grimy with the winter's snowy sludge.

"Let's have a look," Jordan grunted as he pulled himself up onto the rear deck of the truck. He pulled the latch, reefed up on the handle, and the back door rose on rusty pulleys to expose—

"Jesus Christ!" exclaimed the startled union president. "Now what the fuck is this?"

Molly tried—unsuccessfully—to stifle a stoned guffaw. "You said you wanted fish, Jordy, and now here they are."

She and Jake joined Nelson in staring incredulously at the sight that awaited them in the back of the truck—an impossible tangle of fish eyes, fins, tails and gills, all frozen into one huge, impenetrable, ice-encrusted mass.

Nelson was speechless. While he hadn't given the matter a great deal of thought, he'd envisioned a truck load of B.C. salmon—sockeye, maybe even coho—all individually wrapped and neatly encased in plastic, but this ...

The fish distribution was scheduled to begin in the morning, and the union president fully expected his members to begin lining up before dawn, drawn by the ever-powerful lure of getting something for nothing, word of the Fishermen's Union's generosity having travelled far and wide.

They had maybe five hours to get this thing figured out.

Jordan led the group, minus the courier, back up to his office, muttering to himself the while. " ... three hours time difference ... maybe I'll get lucky and they're working late out there ..."

Once he'd settled behind his desk Nelson reached for his Rolodex, the circular card file that held a record of names and contact information. Jordan's had at least doubled in size since the strike began.

As Molly and Jake looked on in bemused silence, the union president punched in what was clearly a long distance number.

"Yeah, George, it's Jordan Nelson from Sudbury calling ... just wanted to thank you for all that, fish, brother."

"Yeah, the truck just got here, and I wanted to ask, what kind of fish is that?"

"Now listen, the driver said something weird, that he had to keep the reefer running, but listen, George it's never warmer'n twenty below here right now so I don't see ..."

"Huh! Is that right? Uh huh, I understand. Okay, brother, it's getting' kinda late here, but we just wanted you guys to know you fed many a Sudbury family, all right?"

"Yeah, well, I can promise your generosity won't be forgotten, okay George? All our best to you and your members out there, brother.

"Merry Christmas to you, too, man," and with that Jordan cradled the phone on his desk before looking at Jake and Molly, who were watching—and listening—in expectant silence.

"Herring. It's herring. He says they had a pretty good run of it this year. And he also said the truck has to be kept running—even in this cold—because if the fish do ever begin to thaw out, they'll begin to thaw at the centre, and then from the inside out ... "

" ... now, we gotta figure out how we're gonna distribute this stuff ..."

Nelson swiveled in his office chair to reach into the pocket of the winter coat that was hanging on a coat rack behind him. He pulled out a set of keys, selected one, and offered the ring to Jake. "Here, Jake. You've been to my house before. Here's the key to the front door. Downstairs in the basement is a workbench. My chainsaw's sitting on it. There's a can of mixed gas right beside it. Can you bring them both down here to the hall, please?"

"Sure thing," Jake nodded, rising to his feet and heading for the door.

"Oh, and Jake? Almost forgot. If you look in the kitchen you'll find a bunch of plastic shopping bags wedged in between the cupboards and the fridge. Bring those, too, will ya?"

"You got it, Pontiac," agreed Jake, who was already halfway out the door, keys jingling in his hand.

The whole thing was a nightmare from start to finish, and was destined to become one of Jordan Nelson's worst memories of the strike.

It didn't help that he was sleep-deprived. He'd decided to pull an all-nighter (just one of many during the Year of the Long Strike, when he sometimes felt obliged to act as an ever-watchful sentinel, standing lonely vigil over the sleeping masses, peaceful in their respite from the terrible, unending struggle over which it was his duty to preside.)

Jordan had sent Molly and Jake home for the night, and he was just settling in in his office chair to grab what little sleep he could when he heard an insistent rapping at the door.

"Jordan? Mister Nelson, sir?"

The voice, a timorous wheedle, Nelson recognized as belonging to Bill "Shakey" Akerley, the Hall custodian.

"Yeah? What is it? Oh c'mon in, Sha—uh, Bill," the union president answered wearily.

The janitor, looking as disreputable and disheveled as ever, slouched through the door frame. As usual, he had no teeth. As a result his words were slurred, and also as usual, he had difficulty making eye contact with Jordan, which only enhanced his disreputable, furtive air.

"Well, Mr. Nelson, sir, remember how you told me that there reefer out back had to keep running at all times?"

Jordan nodded.

"Well, sir, she's stalled right out, not running no more. I just thought you'd wanna know, sir." The tall, white-haired Akerley was clearly distraught at being the bearer of such bad news, and almost despite himself Nelson's heart went out to this lost and lonely midnight apparition with his shock of unruly white hair and thick white eyebrows.

"What? Oh, okay, Bill, I'm coming." Feeling about as old and disheveled as the Hall janitor looked, the much younger man heaved himself out of his comfy warm office chair before beginning to bundle up once again for yet another foray out into the perishing cold.

"You did the right thing, Bill, coming to get me," Nelson reassured Akerley as they trudged down the stairs to the back door.

As it always did not matter how many times he'd experienced it, the fierce cold came as a terrible shock to Nelson. The instinctive reaction was, always, to recoil, to hunch one's shoulders, to duck one's head, as a turtle might withdraw into its shell at the presence of danger.

But Akerley was right—the truck had stalled. And he'd done the right thing by alerting Jordan as quickly as he had. Diesel-powered motors are notoriously balky in severe cold weather. All Nelson could do as he pulled himself up in to the cab was hope the engine hadn't completely cooled down. The starter motor squealed in protest when Nelson turned the ignition switch, but it turned the engine over once, twice, and then to the young union president's immense relief, the diesel engine itself sputtered back to life.

The shivering duo retreated at once to the warm sanctuary of the hall. They parted on the first floor—Akerley to his cleaning duties, Nelson to his solitary vigil, but only after checking his watch. Three o'clock. He knew what was coming, and trudged tiredly back up the stairs to his office to brew a fresh pot of coffee.

New York City likes to boast that it's "The City that Never Sleeps," but really, in its much more modest way, Sudbury, Ontario Canada is, and always has been, just such a place. It is, for one thing, an early rising place, a metropolitan centre geared to a continuous production cycle, with shifts changing endlessly three times a day, 365 days per year. As a result, the principal streets are almost never completely empty, with off shift stragglers wending their weary ways home even as the incoming shifts leave warm beds to catch an early cage. And so it came as little surprise to Jordan Nelson when he heard the slamming of truck doors and the stamping of winter boots at five in the morning. Expecting to find rank-and-filers eager to collect their catch of the day, he was pleasantly surprised to discover that the newcomers were scrounges, with Jean Claude Parisé at their head.

"'Mornin' Jordy, we just thought we'd help get some fish to the guys out on the lines," Parisé smiled.

"Oh yeah?" Nelson was pleased at this spontaneous solicitude, and brightened almost despite himself. "Well it sure ain't gonna be what you were thinking—hold on, I gotta grab my saw." He double-timed it back up the stairs to his office.

"It's out back. Okay? Let's go." Nelson, all business and now chain-saw equipped, and wearing rubber mucker's gloves, led the way across the faux-terrazzo floor of the main foyer.

Jordan, after hefting his saw on to the back deck of the truck, clambered up himself to the closed rear doors, which he opened by pulling hard on the frozen canvas strap at the bottom of the door. "Ho-aly fuck, Jordy! What in the name of Christ is that?

"Five tons a' frozen herring, J.P. Get one of your guys to back his truck up?"

And so it began—the next twelve hours were a surreal blur for the union president. Deafened by the roar of the chain saw in such a confined space, his fingers nearly numbed by handling gobs of frozen fish, Nelson was surprised by how quickly the icy mass wore down the teeth on the saw, necessitating frequent breaks for him to stop and re-sharpen the chain. It was tedious, but at least the sharpening sessions forced him in out of the cold, allowing him to remove his rubberized miner's gloves, and to begin restoring the circulation to fingers that, he feared, might be coming perilously close to frostbite.

At first, he tried to at least wrap the still-icy chunks of frozen fish in plastic shopping bags, but as the day wore on he began to simply toss the chunks into the beds of an endless succession of pick-ups, where they landed with a resounding "thunk."

But even despite Jordy's efforts and ingenuity, "the great fish giveaway," as it became known, was a bust. Almost no one was satisfied—this one had received a larger share than that one, and the nearly shapeless masses of fish, held together mainly by ice crystals, was unappetizing in the first place. The scratchy feedback began to reach Nelson that same day, even before he laid down his chain saw for the last time, forced to call it quits out of sheer exhaustion and by the onset of the preternaturally early gloaming that always descended over the Nickel Capital on the shortest days of the year.

What had started thousands of miles away with the best of intentions had, for some reason that Jordy never did fully understand, brought out the very worst in the Sudbury rank-and-file, a kind of crabbed mean-spiritedness in a working class army that was always volatile at the best of times, but that was now, after four months without a paycheque, becoming war-weary and battle-fatigued despite its own militancy.

There were many times that year—and the end of the day of "the great fish giveaway" was one of those— when Jordy, as he closed up the Local Union office and turned the Hall over to Akerley, wondered if they hadn't bitten off more than they could chew.

11

The Kindness of Strangers (2)

For her part, Molly Carruth missed the fish give-away—which she would soon learn about as it became the stuff of local legend—and, in any event, she had troubles of her own, a worry that was clearly shared and etched into the faces of the other Wives who attended the last pre-Christmas Party meeting at the same time Jordan Nelson was sawing his way through five tons of frozen B.C. herring.

"So does anyone think we should cancel?" There was a quiver in the voice of the veteran community organizer as she posed the unthinkable prospect.

There was no answer, but no one looked anyone else in the eye during the brief silence that followed.

"No? Well all right then, so it's decided we carry on." The chairwoman turned to Molly. "Molly, you've been spending a lot of time down at the Union Hall lately, can you tell us what's been going on?"

Molly paused to collect her thoughts before answering. Then she chose her words carefully. "Look, don't get me wrong ..." she began, but then her voice trailed off, at a loss for words.

"So how many presents are down there, Molly?" the community organizer asked gently, as if already sensing the bad news to come.

"Like I said, don't get me wrong, there are some presents down at the Hall, but not nearly enough. There's been some response to the Toy Drive—and as Christmas gets closer the donations seem to be speeding up—and there's definitely been some random acts of kindness. Last week a guy over at 2251 put a cap over the bed of his pick-up and loaded some gifts into the back and headed to Sudbury by way of Elliot Lake ..."

Molly could see the Local Union number meant nothing to them.

"Twenty-two fifty one—that's the big local over in the Sault at Algoma Steel—anyways this guy calls ahead to the Elliot Lake locals at Rio Algom and Denison Mines, tells them the truck's on its way, and they fill it up the rest of the way, and by the time it gets here that truck is crammed with presents!" Molly beams at the group, hoping to soften the hard blow of her bad news somehow, but she sees they are not impressed. Elliot Lake, a major uranium mining camp two hours west of Sudbury, is full of Sudbury miners who have relocated during the strike. No one begrudges them the good money they're making in the dangerous, silica-infested underground works of the uranium mines, but their generosity is to be expected.

A deflated Carruth carried on, "Yeah, so any - ways ..."

"So there's nothing we can do now but stay the course and hope for the best," the community organizer replied resolutely, lifting her chin and looking them each squarely in the eye.

"I just wish there were more of the wives here," offered the shy redhead who rarely spoke up during meetings. All of the heads in the room bobbed up and down in agreement. It was a constant, well-worn theme—although there were thousands of strikers' wives out there in the community, only the same forty or fifty ever attended the group's meetings. "Look, we all know the impact isolation can have on morale in the home. Now my husband comes home and tells me what's going on in meetings, but a lot of the other men don't. So most wives have to depend on the newspapers or television to learn what's going on with the strike."

Local news media coverage of the strike was spotty and wildly unpredictable at best, they all knew, and often coloured by whether the boss in a particular newsroom was pro- or anti-union. The strike had long since badly polarized Sudbury's 160,000 residents, splitting opinion down the middle. Either you were for the strikers, or against them. There was no middle ground—"Which side are you on, which side are you on?" was the refrain of an old union song.

"Isn't there some way to get the message out there to the other wives? We know they'll turn out for the Christmas Party to bring their kids …"

"I've got an idea—why not use the kids, and the Christmas Party, to get word out to those women we never see at our meetings?" queried the community organizer.

"Sure, it's a good idea, but how?" responded the redhead dubiously.

"I know! I've got it!" exclaimed the community organizer. "Why not a comic book explaining the strike at a kid's level? We can stuff a copy into every kid's gift bag, and they'll automatically carry it into the home, and to their mom."

"Ya know, that's not a bad idea," agreed Molly, herself a mother of two school-age children. "My own kids are getting hassled at school—'Your mother's stupid to be off the job and missing out on all that money' and all that kind of playground bully bullshit ..."

"Huh!" snorted the normally placid redhead. "Sounds just like some bosses' kids!"

"Maybe we could deal with this kind of issue in the comic book, too," suggested the community organizer, who could sense the comic book idea was gaining traction. "I may know somebody who could draw such a thing on short notice; nothing fancy, mind you, no full-colour illustrations, just plain, black-on-white pen-and-ink drawings. Colour would cost us a lot more, anyway."

Heads were nodding in agreement all around the room, which the community organizer took to be a consensus.

"Okay then, I'll reach out to my artist friend first thing tomorrow morning ... "

Two nights later, and Molly was once again sharing a fat, acrid joint with Jake McCool and Jordan Nelson in the Union President's office. The Hall was closed for the day, and the huge old building loomed around them, darkened and silent, except for the footfalls of yet another after hours courier driver, who rapped softly on Jordy's office door.

"Jordan Nelson here?" asked the driver, waybill in hand.

"I'm Jordan Nelson."

The driver proffered the waybill, which Jordy signed with his usual hastily scribbled flourish. "Let's go see what we've got," Nelson proposed to Molly and Jake, reluctantly stubbing out the joint, which was now little more than a roach, anyway.

It was déjà vu all over again, a fact not lost on Molly, even as stoned as she was. But there was one major difference from the fish delivery—the size of the truck. This time, it was a full-size, ginormous eighteen-wheeler backed right up to the rear entrance of the Steelworkers' Hall.

"Wow!" Jake marvelled at the size of the thing.

"What, Jordy?" Molly stifled a chortle. "D'ja order more fish?"

The Union President stopped dead in his tracks, and turned a mournful, hangdog gaze on Molly. "That's not very funny, Carruth."

"What's in this thing, and where's it from?" he asked the courier.

"Dunno," the driver answered. "Waybill's kinda weird. Doesn't specify the contents, and shipper's showing only 'Way up north,' whatever that means."

"Huh! Well let's see what we got," grunted Jordy as he raised the frozen rear bars on the back of the van.

He awkwardly opened one of the swinging rear doors, and peered inside, along with Molly and Jake.

"Oh my God!" exclaimed Molly, once she saw the van's contents. Her hand flew involuntarily to cover her mouth, her eyes filled with tears, and her knees began to buckle as she realized she was looking at a tractor trailer load of children's Christmas presents, shrink wrapped and stacked high on wooden pallets. She thought at once of the other Wives, and the sudden certainty that all the worry and anxiety of the past few months was now truly over was almost too much to bear. She stumbled backwards, through the back door of the Hall. She had to sit down before she fell down.

"Can you drop this here?" Jordy asked the courier. "We'll get a buncha guys here to hand bomb all this first thing in the morning."

"Sure thing," agreed the courier amiably.

Jordy closed the doors, and realized for the first time that Molly was nowhere to be seen. "Hey, where's Carruth?" he asked Jake, who only shrugged and pointed back inside the Hall.

The two men then went in the back door, where they found Molly sitting on the stair steps, head in hands, weeping silently, hoping not to be seen by the guys, who regarded her in silent embarrassment.

The unloading process began early the next morning in the pre-dawn bitter cold. Jordan conscripted whatever guys were in the Hall so early, and a kind of "bucket brigade" was established, with presents passed from hand-to-hand, down off the back of the truck, through the back door of the Union Hall, up the stairs, across the foyer, and finally, into the Vimy Room, where the pile of presents was growing impressively.

Soon enough, Jordan realized he had a new problem: where to put all those goddamned presents? They were beginning to overspread the floor space of the Vimy Room, always a busy space during the Year of the Long Strike. Strike voucher distribution was centered there, for one thing, as was any emergency membership meeting, guaranteed to be jam-packed by thousands of increasingly restive hard rock miners and surface workers, thirsty for news of progress in bargaining.

No, clearly the presents couldn't stay there. Jordan thought of the basement instead. Beside the clubroom, there were a number of smaller, unfinished rooms down there. Plans to upgrade the space into an education and training centre had yet to be realized, owing to a shortage in funding. Better down there than somewhere out in the community, Jordan figured. Wherever they were stored, the presents would have to be guarded night and day. Those presents were like gold, and this time of year? Forget it. And so, about mid-morning Jordan ordered the flow of presents re-directed, down the stairs inside the back doors, rather than up. Gradually the myriad of small rooms in the basement each began to fill with floor-to-ceiling presents.

Within hours, the Wives buckled down to tackle the greatest logistical challenge of all: how to distribute Christmas presents to fourteen thousand children? Somehow, a means must be devised to deliver the gifts in an age and gender-appropriate way, and, first of all, an inventory must be conducted of the presents in hand. And so the Wives began to rendezvous at the

Hall to clamber through the basement rooms and to count and sort the gifts that had accumulated with the arrival of the big rig, and that were still arriving. Alice McCool led the way. In the days leading up to the Christmas Party she began to arrive daily at the Hall, working long hours with quiet determination to sort, wrap and label the presents. Was this burst of energy from the group's matriarch some form of attempt at expiation for the wives' sell-out of the strike of '58, even though Alice had played no active role in the back-to-work movement? No one knew for sure, but the community organizer had her own suspicions.

History cast a long shadow over each of them, and, even though they were too young to have taken any part in the disastrous strike of 1958, the Wives of 1978 were determined that history should not repeat itself.

12

The Wives Hold a Christmas Party

By the day of the party the Wives had put their heads together and devised an ingenious method for the present distribution. Children were "streamed" as they arrived—by age and gender—and a clearly labeled table set up in the Vimy Room for each category.

It was, all in all, a riotous affair, one of the first great triumphs of The Year of The Long Strike.

The little boys arriving were instantly galvanized as they entered the Vimy Room, immediately thrilled at the sight of the great open space of the capacious room, the seemingly vast distance of it, and the high, airy ceilings. They clapped their hands in delight, and began to run about like maniacs, gamboling recklessly, heedless of their seemingly imminent and inevitable head-on collisions with more sedate passers-by.

They had all been cooped up indoors for what seemed like an eternity owing to the astounding brutality of the terrible winter, and now, suddenly, they were set free, a boisterous tribe.

For their part the girls were just as amazed at the sight of the huge room decorated for Christmas and crowded with tables overflowing with presents. The girls shrieked in delight in ear-splitting screams that only heightened the general, adrenalized pandemonium.

The news media were out in force, too, with multiple cameras set up on tripods, shooting for the local stations, yes, but also for the big national networks, their sun guns glaring throughout the room, the news crews more than a little curious to see whether the Wives could make good on their seemingly outlandish promise that no striker's child should go without a full measure of Christmas presents in The Year of the Long Strike.

The Steelworkers' Hall was the place to be on that day in the week before Christmas, 1978, the Vimy Room the hub of the entire community. For a few hours, at least, the grim business of the strike, with its mounting privations, was forgotten as beaming parents shepherded their children into the Hall to collect their Christmas presents.

Conspicuous in his absence, though little noticed at the time, was only Jordan Nelson, who had elected to stay away from the Hall. Single and childless and still one of the youngest strikers, the strike leader really didn't feel he belonged at the party. Instead, he remained at home, alone, in the run-up to Christmas, choosing not to answer the phone, which rang incessantly. Truth was, he rather enjoyed the peace and quiet, which gave him time to think, to recharge his spiritual batteries.

And so, Christmas Eve found Nelson in solitary contemplation, nursing a cocktail in front of the Christmas tree in the living room of his apartment. He pulled the plug on the string of Christmas lights that festooned the tree and went to bed early, wondering what the New Year held in store. Knowing what he did, it was hard to contemplate the prospects for the coming year without an almost overwhelming sense of dread.

The Christmas Party (Oryst Sawchuk, 2017)

PART TWO
Winter

13

Lunch Bag Let Down—
and a Surprise Announcement

It was an unthinkable development, even before the holidays, but it happened that year: the weather took a sudden turn, and it became even colder in the New Year. It became so cold, in fact, that the Great Lakes that lie just to the west of Sudbury froze solid, a rare meteorological phenomenon that happened but once in a generation.

This meant that whatever moderating influence the vast open waters of Lake Superior, Lake Huron, and Georgian Bay might have exerted to temper the plummeting temperatures in the Nickel Capital were gone now, the roiling, frigid waters of those huge inland seas replaced instead by limitless sheets of wind-scoured ice larger than a number of U.S. states. The westerly winter winds that normally blew through the streets of the Gatchell, Flour Mill and Donovan districts now packed a hypothermic punch backed by a thousand miles of Arctic, unobstructed fetch. The streets were, in fact, deserted. Pedestrian sightings had become a rarity—few souls were foolhardy enough to brave the cutting winds that made frostbite and even death an immediate prospect. Cars weren't much better. Winter days like this were known in the local vernacular as "square tire weather" because in the unlikely event that your vehicle's frozen battery had enough cranking power left to cause the engine to cough into listless, sputtering life in the morning, the first few hundred yards travelled produced the queer sensation of driving not a modern product of a Detroit assembly line but rather a Flintstones-era conveyance equipped with crude wheels that had been chiseled out of solid stone, and were not smoothly rounded at all, but were somehow out of round. The rubber that touched the roadway overnight had molded itself to the flat surface and the air molecules inside the inner tube were too frozen to expand and fill out the steel-reinforced tire rubber.

The effects of the perishing cold were felt most acutely by the guys on the lines, of course. It was a matter of urgent necessity, pride and union militancy that the picket lines be stoutly manned day and night despite the brutal cold, and each line was equipped with a heated trailer, a barebones, sheet-metal affair, the type of ATCO trailer found on construction sites across Canada. For all its cheerless, Spartan simplicity, the trailer provided a welcome refuge from the biting cold and bone-numbing wind. They were not always, however, a place of warm camaraderie.

Gone now was the ebullient swagger of the early fall, replaced by a thin-lipped look that could have been easily mistaken for dark and utter despair. The

thousand-yard stare. No matter how prudent or prof-
ligate, each man's family had long since exhausted its
savings, and destitution now loomed. At least the
holidays had leavened the bleak, foreshortened days
of early winter with the distraction of carols, cheery
greetings, and the Lions Club Childrens' Christmas
Telethon, an annual fundraising television staple that
was both homespun and heartwarming.

That they were able to straggle on at all was the
result of desperate, ongoing, behind-the-scenes jaw-
boning—some might say intimidation—at the Union
Hall. Fuel oil dealers, prescription-drug and baby-
formula purveyors, supermarket managers, each was
summoned to the Hall in turn to confront a flinty-
eyed Nelson and an ever-glowering Haywire. Which
side were they on? The union leaders demanded.
There was, there could be, no middle ground. Every
weasel-word, each equivocation now is etched in
stone, to be long remembered once the strike was
settled, and it would be settled; today's misdeed
would be remembered once the fat Inco pay cheques
were rolling in again. Supporters now would be
favoured later, vacillators now would be punished—
perhaps even boycotted—forever more. Memories
were long in such matters. One hapless open-line
radio host, who maintained his own staunch neutral-
ity throughout the strike, was discovered by the old
Mine Millers to have been the grandson of a would-
be scab during the great Kirkland Lake Gold Strike
of 1941, which had paved the way for the unionization
of Sudbury in 1944. And anyway, what could be
expected from such a scabby bastard?

On the other hand, the tendons of Sudbury's tightly knit community often held across class lines and Nelson and Haywire were sometimes pleasantly surprised by the responses of local merchants and franchisees. Nelson never forgot the quietly defiant pre-Christmas words uttered to him by the manager of a sizeable supermarket out on LaSalle Boulevard. His bosses, a blue-blooded family of Toronto plutocrats, had authorized him to donate a Christmas turkey to each striker's family. Strictly Grade B, of course. "But there's no way I'm giving a bunch of Grade B birds to a bunch of Grade A customers."

The first Wives' meeting was a reflection of the mood out on the lines. With the excitement and undeniable success of the Christmas Party now behind them, there was a distinctly anti-climactic mood in the room, a sense of some titanic battle having just been won, but also an apprehension that the war was far from over, that another battle lay just ahead. But there was also an underlying sense of emptiness: so, they had done something great. But what did they do for an encore?

The community organizer was in the chair that morning. Acutely aware of the mood in the room, and concerned about it, she hoped to smooth things over by retreating to safer ground. She turned to Molly. "So, what're they saying about us now down at the Hall, Molly, after the Christmas Party?"

Carruth just beamed. As they all knew, the event had been an absolute, unalloyed triumph. In the end, they'd actually had a surfeit of presents, and the surplus had been shipped to a small, struggling Lumber and Saw local fighting a tough wintertime strike out in frigid Thunder Bay. "Wow. Well, what can I say? We're heroes down there." Molly couldn't help but bask in the knowledge that the Christmas Party had been her idea, an awareness she kept to herself. She turned to speak directly to Brenda Joyce. "And you'll never guess who came up to apologize to me after— Eldon Critch! Told me he was sorry about hassling you that day in the Hall. I thought it was very classy of him to do that, Brenda."

The red-headed, shy Joyce, who rarely spoke at these meetings, coloured at this news, and she nodded appreciatively at Carruth's tidings.

"Oh, I have some news, too," smiled Jo Ann Winter-McCool. "Jake and I are expecting!"

This announcement, as sudden as it was unexpected, was met at first with stunned silence, except for Alice McCool's gasp as the Wives' matriarch realized she was about to become a grandmother for the first time. She rose swiftly, and crossed the circle of women—she fairly flew—into the arms of her still-lissome daughter-in-law. Alice was speechless, fighting an unsuccessful battle against tears, as she embraced Jo Ann. Soon all of the women had gathered around Jo Ann and Alice, their usual meeting circle shrunken now into one all-embracing joyous group hug, tears flowing openly as they peppered Jo Ann with questions:

Had she told Jake? What had he said? How far along was she, she sure wasn't showing much yet?

"Yes," "Happy, of course" and "About since the strike started," came her answers, in quick succession.

"So almost four months, then," observed the university professor pensively.

Although none of them realized it at the time, the moment was history beyond a personal measure: for the first time they had begun to measure the strike not in days, or even weeks, but in months.

14

The Mayor Drops a Bomb

Clayton MacKenzie was entering the second year of his second term as mayor—still a relative newcomer—as the strike entered its nadir that winter. A former high school history teacher, MacKenzie was an educated man, a thinker who had read his Machiavelli, which would stand him in good stead in overseeing Sudbury's notoriously fractious City Council. But his greatest asset, he knew, was Daisy Symanzki, his executive assistant. Daisy had served every Sudbury mayor in living memory, and she had shown him the ropes around City Hall, which had only recently moved from its former location in a red brick building on Cedar Street to palatial new digs, Civic Square, on Drinkwater Street.

As he arrived at his office in mid-January, Daisy greeted MacKenzie with peculiar news: a priest from a local downtown parish had just called, wanting him to participate in a prayer meeting of community leaders to pray for a peaceful end to the strike—and surely preciptate it. MacKenzie, crossing through Daisy's anteroom toward his own inner office, stopped short. "Eh, what?"

Daisy repeated her message. MacKenzie frowned. "I don't like it, Daisy. It's a set-up, a sneaky way of starting a back-to-work movement, to get the guys to go back on the job, no matter what, and I'll have no part in that," MacKenzie declared as he hurried past Symanzki's desk, headed once again for his own inner sanctum. The Wives were not the only people keenly cognizant of the lessons of the '58 strike— MacKenzie was not about to repeat the example of his predecessor, who had rounded up the strikers' wives into a mass meeting in the Sudbury Arena at Christmas that year, an opportunistic expedient that had broken the strikers' resolve, the strike, and even, in the end, the union itself.

"No, you don't understand, Clayton. They WANT you to be there."

This stopped the Sudbury mayor dead in his tracks. "You mean he's ordering me to be there?"

Daisy nodded, eyes downcast. "That's about the size of it, yes sir."

MacKenzie's frown deepened into a scowl at such effrontery before his mood changed abruptly. "You know what, Daisy? They want a prayer? Let's give 'em a prayer!"

MacKenzie had long since come to his own personal conclusion about the strike: he hated it, hated what it was doing to his community, hated the way it was driving so many local merchants to the wall, hated the way some strikers were beginning to lose their homes, hated the unbearable stresses the strike was imposing on marriages, which were falling apart in record numbers. There were even dark rumours of an increase in suicides and suicide attempts. But which side was he, Clayton MacKenzie, on? Politically he was a Tory, which should have marked him on the company side of the ledger. But Clayton MacKenzie also counted himself among a dwindling number of a peculiarly Canadian strain of Toryism, a political brand that normally occupied the right side of the political spectrum. MacKenzie was a so-called Red Tory. Strongly communitarian and not averse to a robust nationalism when necessary, Red Canadian Tories were a fiercely independent political tribe, quietly pragmatic and open to compromise, yes, but also as ambitious and covetous of political power as any other Canadian politico, and MacKenzie definitely had ambitions beyond the confines of the Sudbury city limits. He weighed all these factors carefully as he rolled up his shirtsleeves that night at home after work, reached for a tablet of foolscap, and sat down to write.

The finished product, which he'd read aloud as he wrote it out longhand in the evening quiet of his basement rec room, timed out to about forty-five minutes. He took it in for Daisy to type up and copy the next morning.

"How many copies will you be needing?"

"Oh, not that many. Just one for every reporter in the room."

Mayor Clayton MacKenzie paused at the entrance to the big room, to scan the spectacle he was about to enter. The grand ballroom of the Holiday Inn in downtown Sudbury really was a big room—and one of the city's most expensive. MacKenzie took in the reporters waiting impatiently for the show to start— a loosely clustered semi-circle at the back of the room—and the assembled clergymen, seated in their own, facing semi-circle on the raised dais at the front of the room, and, as if to confirm his own most suspicious conspiracy theories, there, right in their midst—Cam Newton, the Ontario Division President of Inco!

MacKenzie made a quick study of the religious at the front—their denominations, their neighbourhood church locations. His was not a particularly religious community—church attendance was down all over town, and the strike was especially ruinous at the offertory—which brought him back to his original question: who was footing the bill for this little bun fest? His eyes came to rest again on Newton, attired in his conservative dark businessman's suit, sitting motionless in his chair stage centre, directly behind the speaker's podium.

MacKenzie drew a deep breath, put on his best sincerely phoney-as-all-hell smile, and stepped into the maelstrom.

First the Sudbury mayor was careful to work the back of the room, smiling politely, shaking hands with each of the reporters in turn. "Hello,____, good to see you." He knew each of the reporters by name, which station they worked for, the precise ratings each station had achieved in the latest BBM book. "Would you like a copy of my spee… er, prayer?"

For their part each member of the press corps politely accepted the proffered sheets. The tacit consensus on MacKenzie was that he was a shrewd manipulator, verging on a conniver, and too Nixonian by half.

Handshakes and frozen smiles were reciprocated, the niceties observed.

Then MacKenzie crossed the vast, empty open space between the press corps and the religious assembled on the raised platform in the front of the room. He was surprised, and perhaps a trifle disappointed, that the priest who had demanded his presence had not issued an invitation to the public-at-large, and especially the strikers. The company was represented, but not the union, which did seem odd. MacKenzie was concerned to the utmost that the message he was about to deliver reach the strikers and their families.

In this, as it was about to turn out, he need not have worried.

His opening remarks were pure vanilla and about what everyone present expected: greetings, appreciation at having been invited to contribute his thoughts in this most difficult of circumstances.

And he had been thinking about the strike, MacKenzie assured the gathering, had given the matter a great deal of thought. Around him the clergy, with prayerful, downcast eyes, were nodding slightly, and smiling beatifically. So far, so good. The mood was blissful, almost soporific.

The strike had created an almost unparalleled crisis within their community, MacKenzie noted. And how had this come to pass? Just *why* had it come to pass? For his part, the mayor found it hard to fault the union in all of this. The union had not wanted this strike, as evidenced by its willingness to extend the old contract three times—an unprecedented break from its well-established tradition of "no contract, no work," meaning that a strike call was automatic the instant the old agreement officially expired. No, MacKenzie had decided after long and careful—even prayerful—deliberation, the blame lay not with the union, but with the company. Someone, somewhere within the corporate hierarchy had deliberately engineered this strike, heedless of the cost to the community, or the suffering engendered by his decision. It was all a callous decision based on nothing more than cold, calculating corporate greed.

Around him, though he could not see it, the beatific smiles above the clerical collars had begun to freeze, the smiles on a dozen freshly scrubbed and impeccably groomed ministerial faces had turned to subtly pouting moues: what was this? And then, for the first time, MacKenzie heard it: a whispered voice directly behind him, imperious, emphatic: sit down!

The mayor pressed on. There were those who had dared hope that in this, the latter stages of the twentieth century, the company might have turned over a new leaf when it came to dealing with its host communities and corporate communications.

But no, it had now become clear that the morally corrupt old ways still prevailed. "Sit down," came the voice behind him again, louder now, more frantic. Suddenly, MacKenzie realized it was the voice of Cameron Newton, the senior-most representative of Inco in the city. Were it not for the large array of empty chairs that separated the speakers' platform from the news media, at least one sharp-eared reporter would have picked up on the Inco boss's whispered imprecation, which was gaining in amplitude and urgency with each repetition, and which MacKenzie continued to ignore.

But, in the event, only MacKenzie heard the startling demands of the most powerful man in Sudbury, as he at last concluded his prayerfully disguised diatribe.

Newton was, for once, powerless.

MacKenzie's "prayer" concluded the meeting, which ended in stunned silence. Newton wheeled around from behind MacKenzie to confront the Sudbury mayor with a withering glare. "Do you realize what you've done?"

MacKenzie met him with a level gaze. "Oh yes, I know exactly what I've just done."

15

Spook's Return

Foley Gilpin just happened to be in Jordan Nelson's office when word of MacKenzie's remarkable "prayer" first reached the Union Hall.

The veteran newsman, who had shared a house with Jake McCool and Jo Ann Winter before they'd moved out and gotten married, had been prevailed upon by his good friend Jake to drop everything and come to work for the union as an unpaid volunteer propagandist writing leaflets, press releases, and articles for the small, ragtag little newspaper that had been started up by a group of non-union but politically progressive community members eager to somehow support the strikers. The cheap, giveaway half broadsheet little rag was dubbed "THE STRIKE SUPPORT NEWS."

It had been an excruciating decision for the perennially cash-strapped Gilpin, who was struggling to eke out an existence as a freelancer for *The Toronto Globe and Mail*, which styled itself as "Canada's National Newspaper." The strike had afforded him a first-rate running news story—a genuine national story that could last indefinitely—the gift that would keep on giving. But in his heart of hearts Gilpin had always known what he had to do.

All his life Gilpin, a transplanted American, had had an affinity for the underdog. By the time he was asked to write for the strikers—and Lord knows they were the underdogs in this David versus Goliath contest—he'd been living in Sudbury for going on two full decades, and the place, difficult as it was in so many ways, had begun to feel like home. The strikers were his friends and neighbours. How could he desert them now?

Besides, an abiding thirst for social justice was in his DNA. All his life his parents had been passionate advocates for the poor, racial minorities, the dispossessed. While he'd never really asked, Gilpin suspected they were both "security" members of the Communist Party U.S.A. Foley Gilpin was, in a figurative sense, "a red diaper baby," which made him a perennial outlier in the conservative, middle-western world of the Chicago of his youth. He had, therefore, accepted Jake's plea that he become a union propagandist. In the process he'd become a frequent visitor to the office of Jordan Nelson, whom he'd come to quite like and respect.

The two men were huddled, deep in somber discussion about some aspect of the strike, when they could hear a loud commotion outside the thin walls of Nelson's office. The sudden excitement was palpable. Within moments there was a sharp, urgent rapping on Nelson's door, and a striker unknown to Gilpin stuck his head through the door. He was out of breath, though whether from running up the stairs to the second floor or from running a much further distance, or out of pure excitement, Gilpin could not tell.

"Jordy! Jesus, Jordy, did'ja hear what just happened? The mayor just come out for us! In a prayer! Downtown! He just now did it, swear to God! Quick! Turn on the news!"

A startled Nelson did as he was told, and the radio airwaves were filled with breaking news stories of Clayton MacKenzie's sensational prayer lambasting the company while seeking the Lord's blessing on the strikers, their union, and the entire crisis-gripped community.

Both Nelson and Gilpin listened to the news bulletin in wide-eyed wonder, their black mood suddenly dispelled by an unexpected development that did seem truly providential.

He returned the same way he had left the city nearly twenty years earlier—private, transiting through the private air terminus adjacent to the public terminal at the Sudbury Airport.

The place was the same old bunghole he remembered, Buttfuck, Canada. But Jesus, the cold! He hadn't remembered it as being this cold. Of course, after rapid rotations through places like Saigon, Ventiane and Santiago this end-of-the world place was bound to feel desolate. Wet work had become his specialty, and he rather liked it. His briefers back at Langley had explained this mission as succinctly as possible, on the usual need-to-know basis: seems there was a strike underway in the nickel mines, and the boys in the Pentagon were becoming concerned about the alarmingly low levels of the stuff remaining in their strategic stockpiles.

While it was true the war in Vietnam had ended three years earlier, the American appetite for nickel remained insatiable—there was always some new stealth fighter-bomber project underway, and now, a ramped up multi-billion dollar program to build the latest nuclear-powered aircraft carriers.

But those were the big-picture, strategic matters. His mission here was purely tactical: devise some way to discredit the union, undercut its morale, and rupture its supportive relationship with the surrounding community, to bring the strike to an early end at all costs.

All previously attempted measures to this end had proved unavailing, the briefers had told him. The purely hands-off "wait and see" method, waiting for Christmas and mounting privation to take their toll, with disconsolate wives and mothers urging their husbands and sons to end the madness, had failed.

Even working with local clergy to bring the strike to an end through something called "a prayer meeting"—local ministers, especially Roman Catholic priests, had been staunch, dependable Agency allies in the past, both here and around the world—but this stratagem, too had failed, when the city's mayor had crossed everyone up by unexpectedly speaking out on behalf of the strikers during his "prayer."

The twenty-minute car trip in from the airport gave him time to reflect, and slowly, bit by bit, memories of his first mission to this Godforsaken place came streaming back.

It had been a sophisticated, complex black op back then, involving the Royal Canadian Mounted Police, the local Archdiocese of the Roman Catholic Church, the AFL-CIO, the United Steelworkers of America, and even the State Department, so unlike the solo commando assignment he was on now. The objective on his first trip to this frozen wasteland had been to destroy a Communist-led union that might interdict the flow of vital nickel to the U.S. war machine, and in this their efforts had been spectacularly successful—the union had indeed been smashed mere months after his departure. Yet now here he was again, even though the workers had elected to join a supposedly "safer" union. Didn't these crackers get it? Didn't they know when they were beat?

So here he was again, but alone this time, and free to improvise. He wasn't quite sure at first what he was looking for, only that he'd know—and seize on— the opportunity when he found it.

Nelson and Gilpin listened to the news on Nelson's tinny little office radio in dumfounded silence, Nelson, galvanized, pacing the floor of his cramped office excitedly as the veteran newsman leaned impassively against the wall, arms folded over his chest. The mayor's outspoken "prayer" had caused a sensation.

"Jesus, Foley, I never knew MacKenzie had it in him or that he supported us ..."

Gilpin grunted sardonically. "He' playing the long game, is all, Jordy. The man can count."

The union president paused in his pacing to look Gilpin in the eyes, "Meaning?"

Gilpin shrugged. "Meaning he has greater ambitions beyond the mayor's chair, beyond the city limits, and he knows where the votes are."

The union president swallowed hard, and nodded as he digested Gilpin's words. He'd come to value Gilpin's opinions greatly. The newspaperman was a man of the world, very bright, and the rare individual the battle-hardened Nelson had learned he could trust implicitly. A good writer was always an invaluable weapon in the war, nearly as important as a good lawyer. Except that with most lawyers there was always talk of billable hours, and with Gilpin there was none of that—he had volunteered, at no small financial cost to himself.

The two men, one young but aging fast, the other much older, soon exhausted the topic of the Sudbury mayor's future, and they moved on to the next issue that loomed large over their community but over which they had absolutely, infuriatingly, no control—the outcome of labour negotiations in a town a thousand miles to the north and west of Sudbury. Their fate might well hang in the balance there, and they both knew it.

16

Thompson Settles, and Jordan Nelson Makes a Rare Misstep

There's an old riddle among mining men: "Where's the best place to find a new mine?"

"Right next to an old one."

But by the nineteen fifties this ancient adage had pretty much been played out in the Sudbury Basin, site of one of the greatest ore bodies ever discovered, and would-be mine finders had taken their search much further afield. The International Nickel Company especially, with its vast cash reserves and its customers' insatiable hunger for its principal product, led the search far and wide, to hitherto unexplored regions of the vast Canadian land mass, and in the 1950s the company's persistence paid off with the discovery of a promising mineral strike in far northern Manitoba. In fact, a whole cluster of sulphide ore bodies were soon proved up by crews of hardy diamond drillers flown into the empty bush not too far south of Churchill, a port town on the shores of Hudson Bay famous for its polar bears. The massive snow white bruins were a familiar sight in Churchill, especially in the fall, when they would take up temporary residence on the outskirts of town, waiting for the Bay ice to freeze solid enough to support their weight, which could range up to a ton. Other than its polar bears, Churchill was remarkable for one other thing—it was the northern terminus for a rail line that linked it to Winnipeg and the transcontinental main line of the Canadian Pacific Railroad. The grand Western Canadian dream was that Churchill should serve as a northern gateway to the world for prairie grain, and sundry other western exports requiring bulk shipment to world markets. But the dream foundered on one bitter, unalterable Canadian reality: Churchill was not, could never be, a year-round port, and the federal government in far-away Ottawa was reluctant to invest millions in icebreakers and infrastructure to develop its own Arctic. Churchill languished, the promise of its visionary dream unfulfilled.

Though nowhere near the elephantine scale of the company's ore reserves in Sudbury, Inco executives quickly determined the viability of sinking a handful of shafts, and within this cluster a year-round live-in camp soon developed in this unlikely location a twelve-hour drive north of Winnipeg. Fuelled by the rapid growth and expansion of the mines, the boomtown became permanent, and it was given the name of a senior Inco executive—Thompson.

By the late seventies, Thompson, Manitoba had grown into a small city and was well on its way to becoming the third largest metropolitan area in the province, the principal regional hub of northern

Manitoba. The Mine Mill union sent organizers in early, when the place was still a camp, and it soon won a certification vote—but who among the rank-and-file of the new local union had the expertise to negotiate a collective bargaining agreement with an adversary as rich and savvy as Inco? No one did, and the National executive of Mine Mill soon decided to parachute in seasoned veteran negotiators from Local 598 in Sudbury to lead the bargaining on behalf of the newly unionized workers in Thompson. The Thompson Local elected its own bargaining committee to attend the talks in Winnipeg, but, as one of the Sudbury men would tell an interviewer many years later, here things met a snag. The Sudbury veterans were all business, as befitted the seasoned leaders of the country's largest union local, but the Thompson bargaining team was less so. Consigned to life in what was still a mud-rutted, isolated mining camp only recently elevated from bunkhouse living under canvas, the Thompson leadership regarded its sojourn in the big city as an irresistible invitation to indulge in some much-needed R and R, often arriving at the bargaining sessions badly inebriated, if, in fact, they managed to arrive at all. Their Sudbury counterparts, an upright, sober, industrious—but homesick—lot, soon tired of the Thompson gang's shenanigans, opting to settle for the first decent contract offer that came their way, so anxious were they to return home. They gave absolutely no thought to the possible future importance of synchronizing the new Thompson contract's expiry dates with those of the pre-existing Sudbury contracts.

Years passed, and boomtown Thompson evolved into a well-established, prosperous modern community carved out of the northern Manitoba wilderness; the streets were paved and lit, bunkhouses gave way to suburban-style back-splits and side-splits. A short spur line was even built to connect Thompson to the Winnipeg-Churchill railway. The short line stemmed from a lost railway junction just south of Churchill called Gillem. The place—which was really no place, at all—must, however have had its own, unstaffed, remotely controlled Environment Canada monitoring station, as nationally-televised weather presenters would, on rare occasions, dutifully relay news of "current conditions in Gillem, Manitoba," clearly unaware that there was no there there. The Thompson spur, besides providing passenger access to the mining centre, also allowed for a means to ship concentrate from the mills Inco had built at the centre of its clustered mines to the outside world. It was true that the steel rails undulated crazily over the endlessly heaving permafrost of northern Manitoba and that strict load and speed restrictions applied to the locos pulling long strings of concentrate-laden gondolas out of Thompson, but, tenuous as it was, that logistical link allowed at least a trickle of nickel to reach world markets. It was nowhere near the steady stream of throughput that flowed daily from the company's now strike-bound Sudbury operations, but that thin stream of nickel had assumed inordinate importance to Gilpin and Nelson as they switched off the radio newscasts concerning Clayton MacKenzie's "prayer."

MacKenzie's calculated outburst had provided an impromptu shot in the arm to the strikers' cause, but now another threat loomed: would their brother Steelworkers in Thompson join them on the picket lines, or would the members of Local 6166 there settle and continue to bolster the company's bottom line by continuing to contribute, however minutely, to the company's nickel stockpiles?

Once in a lifetime, if you're very, very lucky there may come an electrifying moment like this: suddenly, with very little warning, events will conspire to put you on an island in a crisis where, without thinking, you know, you just *know*, how to lead in that crisis, where four decades of life experience have equipped you, and you alone, to act to control the damage— and the danger—stemming from that crisis. Just such a moment was about to occur in the life of Foley Gilpin.

The shocking news that Thompson had settled burst over the city like a bombshell, and subsequent events moved so swiftly that Gilpin was caught off guard, and at some distance from the centre of the action.

The first fallout began, naturally enough, in the office of Jordan Nelson, in his second floor office in the Steelworker's Hall. It was a logical call to make, once the news came over the wires, for Sudbury newsmen to seek the union leader's reaction.

Though taken aback by developments in Manitoba and deeply dismayed that fellow Steelworkers had elected not to strengthen his own strike, Nelson maintained an outwardly calm reaction. As bitterly cold as it was in Sudbury, it was much colder still in Thompson, so much further to the north. Who could blame a group of workers for avoiding an outdoor picket line in such circumstances?

Besides, Nelson told a radio reporter, the matter had been decided by a free and democratic vote among Inco employees in Thompson, and he was not about to second-guess them.

Had the reporter heard what was in the agreement?

The offer was but a stand-still, three-year agreement, with only the most nominal improvements to contract language, benefits and wages. Did Nelson think the Thompson tentative agreement might serve as the template for a settlement in Sudbury?

Here Nelson paused briefly to reflect, thinking how even such a minimal offer back in the fall could have averted the entire Sudbury strike. He mumbled some kind of affirmation.

The reporter, surprised at this response, struggled successfully to conceal his own reaction, thanked the union president for his time, swiftly wrapped up the interview, and rang off. He had his scoop, which went to air within the hour.

Nelson convened an emergency meeting of his War Council to discuss developments in light of the Thompson settlement that afternoon.

A few of his most trusted advisors had already had the presence of mind to visit the picket lines to gauge rank-and-file reaction to Nelson's public statements, and the union president could tell from the worried looks on the faces around him that they were in trouble.

"You shit the bed, boss, I can't tell ya how bad," was the opening appraisal of Haywire d'Aquire, who spoke with his usual candour. At least no one could ever accuse Jordan Nelson of surrounding himself with "yes" men, reflected Jake McCool.

Haywire had been at the gates of his former plant, the giant Copper Cliff Smelter.

Molly Carruth nodded somberly, sharing d'Aquire's gloomy assessment. The same was true at her plant, the Copper Refinery. "What were you thinking, Jordy? No way we'd ever settle for what Thompson got— we've been on strike for almost six months—and they weren't out for even a day. No wonder guys are so pissed off. What the fuck were you thinking?"

Jake watched the colour drain from Nelson's face as, one by one, his closest friends and confidantes continued to deliver their brutal verdicts. But Haywire still wasn't finished: "And another thing the guys want to know—shit, we all want to know—is why in the hell Thompson's contracts and ours aren't co-terminous? We're all in the same union, ain't we?"

Even Nelson himself had no explanation for this, the institutional memory for the role Sudbury Mine Millers had played in negotiating the first Thompson agreement having been lost, along with much else, during the bitter, inter-union battles between the Steelworkers and Mine Mill. They had lost touch with their own past.

And now, even the most militant and committed members of Local 6500 did not know what they did not know, and that was, quite possibly, the greatest loss of all.

A shaken Jordan Nelson returned to his office as soon as the War Council meeting was adjourned. He found a thick sheaf of pink telephone messages waiting on his desktop. Many were from the media. The union president was shuffling idly through the pile when he found a "please call" message from the radio reporter to whom he'd given the disastrous interview earlier in the day. Thinking, perhaps, to repair the damage he instructed his secretary to place the return call.

The reporter was pleasantly surprised to hear from Nelson, and he hastily put up a tape to record the conversation. Their earlier encounter, as both men knew, had created a sensation, with every newsroom in the city scrambling to "match" the story.

"Yeah, about that, I never meant to say the Thompson agreement would be acceptable to our members."

"But that's exactly what you did say, Jordan, with all due respect."

"No, I didn't."

"Well how do you explain this, then?" The reporter punched a few switches on his control board and rolled a cart machine that contained Nelson's words of the morning.

The union president listened in silence. "I was taken out of context," was the best he could muster.

"That's your final comment on this matter? That's all you have to say?"

"Yes."

"Okay. Jordan Nelson, President of Local 6500, thank you for your time." The radioman's voice was a resonant, confident full baritone that fairly boomed out of the loudspeaker.

"You're welcome." Jordan Nelson's voice, by contrast, sounded weak and thin, almost despondent.

The story broke high, wide and handsome at the top of the next hour. The headline was predictable: "Union President caught trying to lie his way out of embarrassing situation." The report opened with a brief explanation of the first tape and then segued into Nelson's feeble attempt to walk it back. It was bone-crushing stuff, and Foley Gilpin followed the story, like thousands of his fellow Sudburians, on his radio throughout the day. He was especially galvanized by the second report, which he found electrifying in its implications. It seemed to him that the entire outcome of the strike might hang in the balance, depending on what Nelson did or not do next. And he alone, Foley Gilpin, knew what must be done to shore up Nelson's flagging support among the rank-and-file and to salvage at least one surviving shred of his credibility.

Gilpin's mind raced as he made the short drive to the Steel Hall. He believed Nelson was that rarity among elected leaders—a man of abundant empathy and sincerity who was genuinely loved, even adored, by his electors. The narrative that would survive the strike was already germinating: that Nelson, through his brash, outspoken militancy had caused the strike singlehandedly. But to Gilpin this would always seem a gross oversimplification. A strike mandate had carried repeatedly among the members of the big Local when the daunting implications of strike action were already clear. The members had chosen Nelson as the man to lead them and Gilpin, for one, hated to see that delicate, almost mystical bond between leadership and the rank-and-file destroyed over the course of a single afternoon.

He arrived dry-mouthed and breathless with excitement outside the union president's office within minutes. "Is he in? I've gotta see him right away," Gilpin motioned at the closed door to Nelson's office.

Angel Houle was holding the fort as the President's secretary in the absence of his regular secretary, a much older woman.

"He's in, but he's not having a very good—"

Gilpin bolted for the door before she could even finish her sentence.

"—like I said, go right on in ..."

"Jordan, we gotta talk," Gilpin began the minute he was through the door. The union president sat alone behind his desk. He regarded Gilpin with a silent, dolorous gaze. The newspaperman thought he'd never seen Nelson look so haggard.

"Yeah? About what? It's too late for—"

Gilpin cut him off. "Nah, it's not too late. So you fucked up. Everyone does sooner or later. But there is a way out..."

Nelson regarded Gilpin in dubious silence, but he was listening, as Foley steeled himself to deliver the punch line that would not be popular: "Ya gotta tell 'em ya fucked up, man. Tell 'em you're sorry. They love you out there, Jordan, and you know what? They'll respect you for being honest and they will forgive you."

The union man swallowed hard and said nothing, but Gilpin could see that the wheels were turning. Why was it that men of high station found it so hard to publicly acknowledge their own mistakes and to apologize for them?

Stubborn pride, certainly, that came, Foley reckoned, from reading their own press clippings, always a fatal mistake. But here, now, in this little shitbox of an office with its cheap imitation wood-paneled walls Gilpin saw a different kind of leader emerging as Nelson grappled with Foley's words. Long moments of silence ticked by as Nelson contemplated Gilpin's advice. Finally, the union man emitted a weary, exasperated sigh. "Okay, brother, where do we start?" Gilpin had often enough heard Nelson use the familial diminutive when addressing Haywire and others around the Union Hall, but it was the first time he had ever addressed the newsman in such a way. He felt surprised at the pleasure he felt from the warm, almost intimate tone from Nelson.

Gilpin reached for the sheaf of pink phone messages.

He found what he was looking for almost at random during an otherwise routine drive from central Sudbury out to Levack along Highway 144, just north and west of the city outskirts.

His plan had been to visit the picket lines in Levack, an exercise he'd been conducting since his arrival in the city a few weeks earlier. He'd dropped by all the lines, casually, unobtrusively, just to hear what the guys were saying, searching, always for the slightest opening, the merest chink in the union armour.

That he was able to conduct such an operation at all was owed in no small part to the remarkable change in his appearance since his last sojourn here some fifteen years earlier. Gone was the buzz cut hair and military bearing that bespoke an individual with a strong military background. In its place was a shaggy, bearded appearance that rendered him nondescript on a 1979 Sudbury picket line.

He owed this change in appearance to his last assignment, that was not Agency at all—at least ostensibly—but was to a newly created, crack combat unit of the U.S. Navy known by an acronym that described its varied theatres of operation—Sea, Earth, Air, Land—or Navy SEAL, for short. It was an assignment that suited him down to the ground—functioning as part of an elite combat squad so dark it often verged perilously close to being beyond the bounds of normal military discipline. They were a band of killers, rigorously trained and superbly equipped, trained especially to hunt, and kill, in a pack.

And nowhere did the relaxation of normal military discipline apply more than in the area of personal grooming. In what could have been seen as a backhanded compliment to the generation they collectively detested, they cultivated long hair, beards and moustaches, all of which made it easier to fit in when working undercover assignments to infiltrate the plethora of youthful underground revolutionary organizations that had sprung up during the nineteen sixties and seventies—outfits like the SDS, Students for a Democratic Society, AIM, the American Indian Movement, and the Black Panther Party. Strictly speaking such domestic surveillance was the proper and exclusive bailiwick of the FBI, but it was a free for all back then, with federal agencies competing shamelessly for turf, as he'd learned when, during one of his infrequent returns to Langley, he'd been thoroughly debriefed about his experiences training and serving as a Navy SEAL. Only then did he realize his secondment was intended as a deep penetration of the elite new killer squad. The Agency's appetite for intelligence, even on branches of its own government, was, it seemed, insatiable. How had Angleton put it? The crusty, crafty old James Jesus Angleton, long-time head of counterintelligence, had once famously quipped that, "Penetration begins at home."

And speaking of penetration, that was one of the many bennies that came from working the beat beat. Man, those hippie chicks loved to put out. Not like those cock-tease cheerleaders in high school who'd driven all the players on the football—himself included—to distraction. No, the young women who flocked to the Movement were experienced, not shy, and, best of all, on the pill, so you never had to worry about knocking one of them up.

Such dalliances, combined with the necessity of being psychologically and physically prepared to deploy anywhere in the world on twenty four hours' notice, running deep and dark for months at a time, if necessary, took a heavy toll on SEAL marriages, which failed ninety per cent of the time, with wives not knowing where their husbands were, left alone to head the family, always fearful their children's father might return home in a box.

But still, for the adrenaline junkies they all were, there truly was, in the words of the army recruiting video, "no life like it." The bonds of brotherhood, the sense of being part of an elite team with a license to kill, was the ultimate kick. He preferred not to dwell on the earliest tell-tale signs—already becoming apparent—that many of his fellow commandos were damaged goods, deeply troubled for life by all that they had done and seen.

17

Tipping Points

Foley Gilpin had never, particularly, been a devotee of Karl Marx, but when he discovered that at least one Econ course was a prerequisite for his journalism degree back at Northwestern he'd opted for a course called "Introduction to Marxist Economic Theory," overall a rather dreary affair, but one particular tenet of Marx's theory had intrigued him: Marx's notion that capitalism's undoing would ultimately stem from the contradiction between the relations of production, where plants and factories were in private hands and the mode of production which was highly socialized, with thousands of workingmen unwittingly organized by the bosses to labour in coordinated fashion, across a multitude of skills and disparate workplaces, to produce a single, value-added product.

The workers would, Marx predicted, learn from this on-the-job organization, and begin to band together in other ways, fighting for higher wages and better working conditions. Soon such demands would bloom into contention about overall control of the means of production, and calls for all-out revolution would be heard.

And it must have seemed the first seeds of Marx's predictions were coming true in his lifetime when, in the 1850s, the workers in English industrial concerns were beginning to organize themselves into unions along craft lines. The first calls for collective bargaining and higher wages were heard, even backed occasionally by work stoppages, infuriating the owning class, which called in, often as not, the police. Scabs were also commonplace, recruited from the ranks of the unemployed, a perennial underclass Marx described as "the reserve army of labour."

To Gilpin, it seemed that the imposing edifice at the corner of College Street and Frood Road was now ordered as an illustration of Marx's point on labour and the mode of production in modern industry. Just as Marx had prophesized, the bosses had unwittingly taught the workers how to organize. And it was all happening with astonishing speed before Gilpin's incredulous eyes. The strikers seemed to know instinctively what needed to be done, and how to band together, almost without thinking, without even speaking, to accomplish the task at hand. They were a practical, resourceful people, after all, backed by the vast resources of the million-plus North American members of the United Steelworkers of America, and, thanks to the International Nickel Company they were now well and truly organized.

Strikers' families were finding it difficult to put food on the table? Organize a food bank. Mothers worried about dressing their children warmly enough to withstand the potentially lethal playground cold of that terrible winter? Here the Wives' support group rallied to the cause, and a clothing depot was established, to collect and distribute warm winter clothing. Like schools of fish, Gilpin watched as thousands of strikers and their wives swirled about, coalesced around an urgent task, and then swam on. And in this constant churn there developed an incessant appetite for situational leaders. And here again the raw, heretofore untapped resources of the Sudbury rank-and-file appeared almost inexhaustible. The lowly grade-two dropout sweeper from the smelter shop floor—a functional illiterate in both official languages—suddenly discovered a natural bent for running a food bank, and for the first time in his life people began to look up to him. Dozens, even hundreds, of people were suddenly discovering their true calling in life for the first time, and it had nothing to do with producing nickel. But so electrified, so enamoured were they by this sudden onrush of new responsibility that they arrived at the Hall earlier, and stayed later, each day. They never missed a shift. It was heady, even addictive, stuff. And in this way new names, whole new reputations, soon began to bubble up from the first floor of the Hall, to the second floor, where the Local 6500 leadership was ensconced, and even all the way up to the topmost, third floor, where the International Union Staff Representatives, men plucked from the local union leadership ranks by Pittsburgh for full-time jobs with the union, were quartered.

It was a time of swirling, galvanic energy, as future new leaders were thrown up from the heretofore nondescript rank-and-file membership. All in the blink of an eye, and in this way the future of the big old Local was renewed and, even in this most parlous of times, secured.

And nor was this phenomenon limited to the city limits of Sudbury. By this time in the strike the Road Trips Committee envisioned by Jordan Nelson seven months and a lifetime earlier was up and running, dispatching bands of strikers to make speeches and drum up support all over Canada. These Sudbury rank-and-filers were astonished to discover that, wherever they went, they were lionized by trade unionists everywhere. John Lennon was right: a working class hero was something to be. The Sudbury strike had morphed into a national *cause célèbre*.

The strike also achieved notoriety through news media reports that it had, just days earlier, become "the longest strike, in person/days lost" in the annals of Canadian labour. To some, this was a dubious distinction, while to others it was worn as a badge of honour. The record was broken due to the tremendous multiplier of the sheer numbers of striking workers— there had been longer strikes in Canada, in absolute terms, but none involving so many strikers.

On his return from the lines at Levack, he slowed down to do a closer visual of the place he'd spotted on the way out.

He'd learned little from the trip, except that it was nearly the end of March, and the picketers were aware the date meant the end of another business quarter. All were keen to see the Company's Q1 financials, which should reveal what impact the strike was having on the bottom line.

The end of March in this Godforsaken place. What a joke. The days were getting noticeably longer, it was true, but it was still frickin' cold with a dampness that went right through you. And it was gray everywhere, the leaden sky bleeding into the dirty snow that lay over everything. The high snow banks that lined every roadway were gray too, gray and ragged with the winter's accumulated road grit and the toxic emissions from a million passing tailpipes. By now enough road salt had been spread over all the streets and roadways that the stuff congealed into a thin white film that clung to every wheel well, tire and rocker panel, silently turning every metal surface it touched to rusty dust. The stuff was visible on his boots, and the cuff of every pant leg. No matter how often he showered, he felt more salt-encrusted than Barnacle Bill the Sailor.

He slowed as much as he dared, and took in every detail of his target. Ideally, he'd have liked to walk around it for a closer look, but that was far too risky, in broad daylight, adjacent to a busy two-lane highway. No, clearly this would be a nighttime operation, requiring proper attire and the liberal application of faceblack.

What he was able to make out in his quickie recce was an eight-foot-high chain link fence topped with barbed wire around the perimeter, high voltage lines running in from the north, the usual metal-cased stepdown transformer topped by standard brown ceramic insulators that shielded the output lines that ran to the south, over the highway and towards the city, providing high voltage alternating current for lights and all manner of essential services to properties in the city that lie just to the south. He'd no idea just what and who would be affected by what he was about to do, and he didn't particularly give a fuck.

He would be back.

A striker's life. You rose early, because that's when day shift started, and it was by now deeply engrained in your metabolism. Check to see your picket schedule, a complex affair that compassed the normal, workaday three-shift schedule. The schedule was posted in that most public of places, just as his work schedule would have been: the refrigerator door, affixed with a fridge magnet, the closest thing the family had to a bulletin board.

Besides picket duty, there was the myriad of other sundry union meetings necessitated by the strike. As he watched the coffee brew, still sleepy-eyed and stuporous from sleep, he mentally ran down the checklist: not Voucher Day, check. None of the committees he'd volunteered for were meeting this day, check. Just another day on strike, what was it? Number 175. He sighs, looks out the kitchen window in the forlorn hope he'll see some first early sign, even the merest lightening of the sky over the subdivision, an earnest desire that day is, at last, approaching. Still nothing. He sighs again, contemplates the blankness of the day ahead. He feels numb, like some dumb animal consigned—cursed even—to moving in an endless circle, moving, head down, by placing one foot in front of another. The union has coined a hopeful mantra for life on this wheel: One day Longer, One Day Stronger. But he isn't buying it. He isn't feeling any stronger. It is one more day in this terrible war of attrition, and it is getting personal. There may be nothing personal for the faceless suits who have started this war. To them it's all about the numbers they're forever tapping into those fancy newfangled pocket calculators they're always whipping out of their briefcases. And they're still getting paid. But to him and the faceless thousands of others like him out there on the lines, this thing has long since gotten personal. Six and a half months now without a paycheque? What the fuck was that? The Company, certain that sheer, always-dependable human greed will have taken hold by now, is beginning to wonder if it has calculated this thing correctly. How could any of its employees last this long without a paycheque? Surely they would be starved out, bled white, by now, and it's true every family, his included, has long since expended every penny in every bank account. They all are, by any reckoning, dead flat bust.

But what the suits in Manhattan, Mayfair and Bay Street have failed to reckon is the sheer bitter determination and resourcefulness of these Canadian people. Generations of life here On the Rock, with its bitter winters and gritty industrial outlook, the barren, treeless sulphur-blackened rock that has begun to look like home, all of this has, over a century of production, combined to create a new breed, equal parts English and French, part Indian, inured to hardship in a hostile living and working environment. And it is one thing to force them out of the workplace, quite another to get them back into it.

After half a year of this they have devised a host of ways to live without money, chiefly they take care of each other. They have among themselves every industrial skill necessary for survival in the modern industrial age. The men of this place have long since mastered the use of sheer motive force—internal combustion, hydraulics—to move greater weights, arguably, leveraging the muscle of the human body, the power of the human brain, to drill, blast, grind, crush and lift more weight than any other group of men in human history. They are not supermen, but they have, over generations, evolved into a special, unique and generally unsung breed of men. Karl Marx again: "Mankind thus inevitably sets itself only such tasks as it is able to solve, since closer examination will always show that the problem itself arises only when the material conditions for its solution are already present or at least in the course of formation."

So what would it take to end this? He doesn't know for sure, but he knows this much: the asking price for a settlement is now way, way higher than it was when they began. The coffee is ready. He reaches for his mug and heaves another sigh, running his hands through hair still matted from sleep. He looks out the window once again. There is still no light to be seen at the end of this tunnel.

The darkness here suits him just fine; it's when he does his best work. He's parked his car on a side road adjacent to the highway to avoid any unwanted attention, hiking through the snow the short distance to the small, chain-link fence enclosed perimeter.

He slips in behind the fence, away from the highway. Unlimbers the heavy-duty wire cutters. Snip snip, drops to all fours, shimmies on his belly, and he is through the fence, under it.

He removes the C4 from his backpack. The stuff always reminds him of the Play-Do he'd played with as a kid, but this is no toy. He kneads the dry gelatinous substance carefully, into the desired shape, which is to say into a roughly circular lump about the size of a quarter. He slaps it into place against the metal transformer casing. It adheres to the smooth dry surface, even though it is vertical. He removes a coil of igniter cord from his pack and unwinds it, sticking one end to the sticky, gelatinous mass of the G4. Still crouching, he moves around to the front of the transformer, carefully paying out the igniter cord so that it remains imbedded in the charge but with just enough gentle tension that it doesn't touch the snow. He's on the highway side now, crouched low, breathing slightly heavily from the exertion, his back against the transformer wall, the squat massive bulk of it between him and the charge. He lights the end of the igniter with the BiC lighter he always carries and the cord burns its way, slowly, dependably around the corner of the transformer and out of sight. Here there is a delay as it burns around the other corner to its destination. He braces himself, his muscles rigid

148

with the tension of waiting, and his weight is transferred through his legs and torso so that his back is braced tightly against the metal side of the transformer. He feels the thing lift and shake slightly despite its enormous weight. There is a noise, a kind of muted "Whump!" and a sudden flash of light, but both are absorbed harmlessly by the snowy hill that flanks the highway. Then there is the concussive blast wave that radiates through the air until, at some great distance, it will be dissipated, and absorbed into thin air. All very harmless, and Bob's your uncle. Just the way they'd drawn it up back in SEAL training. All very harmless, except for the jagged hole, about the size of a quarter, that has been blown through the heavy steel casing of the transformer and through which a thick viscous oil has already begun to drain. It will take a good half hour, he calculates, before the coolant has drained sufficiently to cause the transformer to overheat, melt down, arc over, and short out, plunging a good portion of the city just to the south into sudden darkness, including a hospital emergency room where a pair of trauma surgeons are working feverishly to save the life of a patient whose internal organs they have just exposed by steady, skilful incisions. But all of this will not happen for another thirty minutes, and he reckons it will be morning before city Hydro crews and the police are able to trace the source of the blackout to this transformer station, and by then he will be long gone. During the detonation he has kept his eyes on the traffic—what little there is of it at this hour of darkest night—his hour. He retraces his steps, drops to all fours, and, in preparing to crawl on his belly back through the hole in the fence he receives the first nasty surprise of the whole op. What the fuck is this? The sudden shock of it takes his breath away. There is icy water beneath the snow.

In the minutes it had taken him to blow the transformer it has begun to thaw.

PART THREE

Early Spring

18

The Gang That Couldn't Shoot Straight and Heartening News from the Financial Page

Throughout the 1970s the Sudbury District was undergoing a period of municipal amalgamation that would transform not only the form of local, municipal governance, but also the company's control over it. Until then, Sudbury was a loose amalgam of outlying small, mainly company-owned towns surrounding the urban core, that is, Sudbury proper.

The smaller towns, places like Coniston, Levack, Copper Cliff and Garson, were company-owned, lock, stock, and barrel. Holdovers from the nineteenth century pattern of mining development when miners' "camps" would spring up adjacent to mining properties or company smelters. Originally little more than a ramshackle collection of tents and muddy streets, the "company towns" had, by the 1970s, morphed into small towns of modest workers' housing—vinyl siding now covered the tarpaper—that boasted the usual urban amenities—running water and sewage systems. But the land they sat on, and the structures themselves, belonged to the company, or at least the company's real estate arm, which had been incorporated as a wholly owned subsidiary to oversee the collection of rents and other fees. The company also controlled the "elected" town council, the local merchants, and even the town police force, which was charged with investigating fatalities on company property, with results that can well be imagined. But by the 1970s the Company was ready to loosen its iron grip and feudal style of governance. It was expensive, for one thing, requiring a battery of property managers and overseers, and even urban planners, who did not contribute directly to the core business of extracting nickel, copper and precious metals.

Coincidentally or not, the Company's desire to move on happened to overlap with a provincially mandated order to amalgamate small Ontario towns into larger municipal units, and so Coniston, Levack and Garson were folded into larger, new municipalities, along with adjacent small towns. The resulting larger municipal structures were assigned new, bland, neologistic names like Nickel Centre, Lively, Valley East, and Walden, place names without either roots or history. There was, in theory at least, one salutary result from this spate of new combinations: the emergence of a new, much larger regional police force availed of the latest investigative technologies and techniques and free at last of the smothering mania for control by the local nickel mining giants, and it was this force that was mobilized to investigate the cause and source of the mysterious and sudden power blackout of the night before.

And so, the very next morning, a small group of sombre men in dark suits, converged on the power transformer that Spook had exited only hours before. They wore galoshes below their long, dark overcoats that did not entirely conceal their fat bellies. The power blackout was a sensational overnight development in a metropolitan area of 160,000 hardwired into the drama of a labour dispute that had paralyzed its economic life over the course of the most severe winter anyone living could ever remember.

Just as Spook had intended, it was widely assumed around town that this apparent act of sabotage was somehow strike related. There was a rich history of striking miners blowing things up, after all, dating from an earlier century when members of the old Western Federation of Miners in Idaho's Coeur d'Alene country had driven a dynamite-laden train into the smelter of the Bunker Hill and Sullivan mining company, blowing up the smelter/concentrator to smithereens. (At the time (then) it was the world's largest and said to be worth $250,000.)

Closer to home, striking Steelworkers in the town of Timmins, a venerable gold mining camp a three-hour drive north of Sudbury, had dynamited the skeletal frame of a high voltage tower carrying power to their workplace in a show of displeasure at the slow pace of negotiations. But those lines had affected only their employer, and the sabotage had been carefully planned to take place far from town, where the power lines running from hydroelectric dams far to the north were remote and highly vulnerable, a long snowmobile ride outside of town.

None of this was lost on the small band of men stamping about impatiently in the snow, awaiting the arrival of a Hydro crew to unlock the gate to the burned out transformer. Although it was still the middle of the night, it was not fully dark. Lowering clouds reflected an eerie orange glow that emanated from the southeast, accompanied by a constant noise from the same direction—a steady growling roar. The light was from the blazing floodlights in the yard of the Copper Cliff smelter, which burned all night long. The noise, which was clearly nearby, also never stopped. The overall effect, rather unsettling, was of some huge, malevolent thing, lurking unseen just over the horizon. The senses were further assaulted by the distinct mephitic odour of something gone off, like eggs rotting or swamp gas. The smelter, and its sulphur-blackened surrounds, had once been described as "The Land of Mordor" from the Lord of the Rings, a comparison that was not entirely inapt.

There was an occasional murmur of discontent to be heard in the pre-dawn stillness from the small, impatiently milling throng.

"So where the hell is he?"

"Late again, as usual. Still running on Indian Time."

They turned to watch a vehicle approaching from the direction of town, a four-door, late model Chevy without hubcaps. One of their own.

Although it had approached at some speed, the driver was now slow to emerge. At length a tall, dark figure shouldered open the driver's side door. He, too, was wearing a long, shapeless dark overcoat and a fedora pulled down low over dark brown eyes.

He touched the brim of his hat in greeting. "Boys." They nodded in return. "Sir." "Lieutenant."

Acting Lieutenant Curtis Southwind, of the Criminal Investigation Branch of the newly formed Sudbury Regional Police Department was now in the house, and clearly small talk was not his thing.

"So whadda we got here?"

A rookie volunteered an answer. "He approached from over there, sir, cut a hole through the fence here, and gained access."

The big man grunted by way of affirmation, surveying the clear tracks in the snow. Now tell us something we don't know. There were two sets of tracks disappearing off into the distance, one presumably as the suspect had made his approach, the second as he had retraced his trail after completing his task.

Southwind pointed in the direction of the disappearing tracks. "Constable, go see where he came from. And for fuck sake don't step on any of those tracks." He hated to part with that many words—especially with that last bit, which should have been painfully obvious—but with raw recruits fresh out of community college, he'd learned, you could never be too careful. Were they really still just the gang that couldn't shoot straight?

The Hydro crew arrived at last, just as the earliest hint of first light began to lighten the eastern sky. As the door through the fence was finally swung open, the men in the topcoats entered the enclosure. They all noticed at once a dark pooling stain in the snow next to the transformer. "Better be careful there," warned one of the Hydro crewmen. "Transformer coolant. Laced with PCBs." The cops gingerly stepped around the black stain. They had all heard about polychlorinated biphenyls, an additive to transformer coolant oil. The stuff was known to be highly carcinogenic. Not something you wanted to track home to the wife and kids.

"He blew it down there." The Hydro worker pointed at a small perforation in the transformer's case just a few feet above the ground.

Southwind, surprised to see how low the hole was, pursed his lips and replied with a characteristic grunt. "Pretty low down, hey?"

The Hydro guy responded with a nod. "He wanted to make sure to drain all the coolant. Which he obviously did."

"Looks like our guy knew what he was doing."

The Hydro worker nodded again, "Oh yeah."

Not the kind of thing your average hard rock miner might know. The small size of the perforation bothered Southwind, too. Not at all typical of a miner's M.O. The old joke around town was about the time the hungry miner went fishing with a lure called a "CIL wobbler," named after the company that manufactured the high explosives in use in Sudbury's mines. The miner tapes together a few sticks of dynamite, lights the igniter cord, flips it over the gunwale, puts his feet up, and waits. The ensuing concussion kills every goddamned fish in the lake, and soon the miner is surrounded by more fish than he can eat, all floating motionless around him, belly up. That was the usual miner's approach. And not for the last time he wonders if it has all been worth it—the terrible environmental destruction—the killing and maiming of so many men in the mines over the years? Just like the Zhaaganash to figure out how to harness technology to go places deep in the earth to release a snake there without first thinking through how to tame that snake. Maybe his elders were right and these children playing with fire lived on borrowed time, doomed by their own disrespectful foolishness to walk the earth for only a brief time before disappearing forever, leaving only the Anishnabek people in this place, balance and harmony once again restored.

There was one on every picket line, and in every picket shack. And likely dozens in attendance at every strike-related membership meeting, when the turnouts numbered in the thousands, as opposed to the uneventful monthly membership meetings, when attendance dwindled to a few dozens, representing a rank-and-file membership of thousands.

These were the rare few who had, for some reason, acquired the arcane gift of analyzing the company's quarterly financial statements, published roughly two weeks after the conclusion of the previous quarter. The Ontario Division Inco first quarter financial results for 1979, which were released in mid-April of that year, made for some riveting reading material in the picket shacks, where these amateur sleuths, scattered throughout the company's far-flung operations in the Sudbury Basin, now began to pore over the dense and esoteric Q1 financials, even as Curtis Southwind was poring over the Air Canada passenger manifests for incoming Sudbury travellers he had ordered a subordinate to obtain from the only airline providing passenger service to the Nickel Capital. The gruff, moody dark-skinned police lieutenant was even more ill tempered than usual as he played several hunches at once that led nowhere. He was searching for a male—he was certain of this much, given the oversized boot imprint left in the snowy tracks leading to and from the transformer station—and he was looking for an outsider with a highly unusual skill set not likely to be possessed by a local. His man might have driven into town, it was true, but Southwind's gut told him this was unlikely.

The picket line sleuthing, meanwhile, was yielding more concrete results that both astonished and greatly heartened the strikers. There were always a couple of givens in these matters: the company's accountants and Public Affairs people would contrive to skew the numbers to present the bleakest possible picture during any bargaining year while burying any possible evidence of a strike's impact to reassure jittery shareholders. But even here, the amateur analysts announced triumphantly to their fellow strikers, there was the first solid evidence that the company was, at last, beginning to bleed. It wasn't easy, but they were just able to connect enough bread crumbs to reach a jubilant, inescapable conclusion: the strike was unsustainable, in the short term, from the Company's point of view. They, the strikers, weren't the only ones being bled white by a strike that was now nearly seven months long.

Sudbury being Sudbury, word of this conclusion, despite the Company's artful attempts to conceal the truth, was all over town before lunch. This included the Union Hall, where Jake observed Jordy Nelson on the broad grin. Jake had never seen the union leader looking so mellow. Nelson suddenly seemed years younger, as if the weight of years had been lifted off his shoulders. It was mid-April, the sun was shining over the old nickel mining camp that had been buried so long in a blizzard of hopeless despond, and the snow banks were just beginning to thaw in the sun's still-timorous rays.

Forgotten for the moment was the hard-earned knowledge that, in Northern Ontario, such early spring days were all too often as illusory as the mirage of an oasis in the sands of the Sahara.

PART FOUR

Late Spring

19

Spring Comes to the Lines

But it was spring, and the fine weather held. It was not, to be sure, the full-on spring of more southerly climes, that beloved season that brought with it each day the return of more bird species, the sun-warmed earth beginning to bloom into flower.

No, this was the typical spring of the more northerly regions of Turtle Island—sudden, abrupt, almost violent, as if someone had randomly thrown a switch—but it was no less welcome for all that.

Out on the lines the strikers no longer stood huddled around smoky hardwood fires in old oil barrels, bare hands outstretched for warmth. The scrounges could, at last, rest easy as the daily need to replenish the jumbled piles of wooden pallets that stoked the fires on the dozens of lines were no longer being drawn down.

And a new sight was now seen out on the lines—children. With hypothermia and frostbite no longer posing a risk, increasing numbers of fathers now elected to bring their children out to the lines in the belief that the experience might provide a more valuable lesson than a day's missed school. It was an experience many sons and daughters would never forget, and it would resonate forty and fifty years hence. In this way the strike became a kind of intergenerational struggle, an inverted variant of New World original sin—the labour militancy of the fathers was visited on the sons and daughters.

And, even as things were beginning to thaw on the picket lines, from far to the south in Toronto there came the first early signs of movement in the key log of the log jam in the deadlocked negotiations.

Jordan Nelson was not altogether surprised when the call came, given the intelligence yielded in the Company's first quarter financials. The government's crack mediators had continued to chip away at the Company's bargaining team in private, low key, but persistent meetings in Toronto. Now they were calling with a heads up: the time was approaching when it might be, in their view, at least expedient to have both sides in the dispute in the same city, if not in the same hotel, or even at the same table.

Nelson, in turn, relayed the news to the members of his own bargaining committee, warning them it might be necessary to travel back to Toronto on short notice. There was great relief all around, not least because a little-noticed deadline had come and gone—the sixth month since the strike had begun. Ontario labour law specified that at this point in any labour dispute the employer could demand that its striking union put its last "final offer" to an acceptance vote of the membership—something no one on the bargaining committee wanted to see. In all probability support for the strike remained strong, but the pressures and stresses of living so long without a paycheque were building, too; nerves were frayed, and a kind of mass, spooked hysteria was highly probable once word got out, and it was bound to, of another nasty wrinkle in the "best and last final offer vote" provision: the employer was legally empowered to unilaterally terminate the employment of any and all of its employees without the usual "show cause" proscriptions other than the fact the employee had been off the job for six months. This deadline had passed in mid-March, and the company's willingness to return to the bargaining table made it highly unlikely that it would now invoke the "last offer vote" clause to break the strike. The union bargaining committee members were acutely aware of this threat, and had discussed it among themselves privately on many occasions, though they'd been careful not to mention it in public or in the media to avoid the possibility of panicking the membership. As he made his calls to the individual members of his bargaining team Nelson felt the overwhelming, palpable sense of relief among them that one more potential crisis looming over them had been averted.

Sudbury sky line before the Superstack. (Oryst Sawchuk, 2014)

20

Return of the Boreal

At first, Jake thought it was an illusion. He had first noticed the phenomenon the summer before, atop a highway rock cut north of town. He'd been driving out to visit his parents when he became aware of some scrubby brush—little more than weeds, really— poking up out of the rock.

But now, here it was again, still there, and even a trifle taller than he'd remembered.

By now it had been—what?—seven years since the completion of the Superstack, the colossal chimney designed to waft away the worst of the sulphur dioxide gasses from the Copper Cliff smelter where Jake himself worked when not on strike. Indeed, the titanic, community-wide struggle to force the Company to clean up its gassy effusions had been launched inside the Insatiable Maw of the Copper Cliff smelter, as had Jake's own career as a union leader—he'd become a kind of poster boy for the resistance campaign inside the smelter—and the attendant publicity had catapulted him into public notice, in both the community-at-large and the Local Union alike.*

---

* The story of the Superstack is told in *The Insatiable Maw, Volume 2* of the Nickel Range Trilogy.

169

It was these same gasses that had destroyed the local vegetation, denuding the landscape and burning the sinus passages, throats and lungs of Sudburians for generations. The huge stack, the height of the Empire State Building, was intended to act as a massive umbrella for the Sudbury District, shielding the area from the strongest concentrations of sulphur dioxide gas. It was hard to believe that in so brief a period it could already be having a visibly salubrious impact on local vegetation, Jake thought. The Superstack was perhaps the world's tallest example of the old polluter's maxim that "the solution to pollution is dilution." By lifting the deadly gasses high enough into the stratosphere that they could be borne away by the jet stream (an expedient Jordan Nelson and his fellow members of Local 6500's newly formed Research Committee had warned against as a quick-and-dirty solution) the most visible impacts of the pollution would be transported thousands of miles away to no one knew where, exactly—the Ohio River valley, even Scandinavia? And yet, and yet … there was the scrubby, scrawny brush, clinging to the rock cut, defying all logic and common sense, and as the lengthening days of April 1979 warmed the black rock of the rock cut, it began to show the first, tentative hints of green.

In fact, Jake was witnessing one of the most remarkable reclamations of the natural world from all-out industrial devastation ever recorded. Or rather, he was on the cusp of it. This terrestrial reclamation had not had its origins on land at all, but rather in the water, when marine biologists had begun to study the effects of the fallout from the Copper Cliff smelter on nearby fresh water lakes. They discovered that the intense concentrations of sulphur dioxide gasses in Inco's airborne chimney pollution resulted in a phenomenon they dubbed "acid rain." This precipitation was toxic enough to tip the ecological balance in lakes in a radius of a hundred miles of Copper Cliff, depending on seasonally prevailing winds.

The scientists learned the earliest impacts were on underwater plants, complex eco-systems that had flourished there for untold eons. Mortality quickly made its way up the food chain, until a lake was declared "completely acidified"—and well and truly dead. They were marvellous to look at: what had been thriving little northern jewels were still pretty, their pellucid waters now crystal clear, objects below now visible all the way to the bottom. But these were empty vessels, devoid of all forms of life.

Scientists noticed something else: when it came to tolerating the effects of acid rain not all lakes were created equal. Certain lakes, usually those bordered by limestone, appeared to be more resistant to acidification. The logical inference: the lime leached into the water, offsetting acidity and mitigating PH imbalance. Could this natural phenomenon be reproduced through human agency as a way to mitigate—if not completely reverse—the acidification of northern lakes? Soon freshwater lake biologists began to tinker with the lakes. They introduced lime into the lakes by the barge-full. Water quality measurements revealed an almost immediate reduction in PH. But the remediation efforts were cumbersome and expensive. Far better to address the problem at its source.

Jake was not alone in noticing the first, faint stirrings of the return of vegetation in the Sudbury spring in the post-Superstack era. Bill Lautenbach, a bureaucrat in the Planning Department of the newly formed Regional Municipality of Sudbury, the same new municipal formation that had spawned Curtis Southwind's new Sudbury Regional Police Department. Lautenbach had a technical background, and he had followed the experiments with acidified lakes with keen interest. And, like everyone else in Sudbury's Planning and Economic Development communities, Lautenbach was also acutely aware of the terrible hindrance the city's physical appearance represented. With its outskirts—and even many of its inner-city neighbourhoods—ringed only by grim, barren black rock, Sudbury had long since become a cheap punch line for many a stand-up comedian: "Sudbury—Pittsburgh without the Orchestra"; "We're giving away a door prize here tonight, folks; First prize, a trip, all expenses paid, one night in beautiful Sudbury, second prize two nights in beautiful Sudbury!" But the city's "image" hit a new, all-time low at about the time of the strike when a reporter for Sports Illustrated arrived in Sudbury during a cross-Canada train trip and alighted briefly on the platform of the city's aging passenger station. He took a quick look around at the notorious Elgin Street strip, the city's skid row, across the street, reboarded the train, and described the Nickel Capital in his article as "a whore in a hovel." Whatever else it may have represented, to Sudburians the city meant home, and they were fiercely proud of the place, jokes, insults, and all. But it stung.

Further confounding the city's image improvement efforts was a widely covered visit by the Apollo astronauts shortly before their successful mission to the moon. The true purpose for their visit: to study "shatter cones," a rare geological formation NASA scientists expected the first human lunar landers to find on the moon. (Shatter cones were the result of asteroid collisions, which earth scientists were coming to believe had created the elliptically-shaped crater that was the Sudbury Basin. The same earth-asteroid collision had released such tremendous force that it splintered the earth's crust all the way down to its core, releasing the earth's molten mineral-rich magma, which bubbled up through the fissures, thus creating the fantastic Sudbury ore body.) But here, in Sudbury's lunar landscape, were honest-to-God astronauts, attired in space suits, preparing for their imminent journey to the moon on the one place on earth that most resembled the back of the moon. The cameras rolled, the Apollo astronauts dutifully posed for their photo-op amidst Sudbury's barren black rock. Seeing was believing. The inconvenient truth behind the training mission simply didn't fit into a ten second sound-bite or a television news reporter's fifteen second stand-up or the back of a matchbook. Seeing was believing. And the camera didn't lie. The damage to Sudbury's image and reputation was international, incalculable. But Bill Lautenbach and his plucky colleagues in the Planning Department simply refused to throw in the towel. What if Sudbury's barren landscape could somehow be forced to regenerate itself? Could the liberal application of lime to restore aquatic flora and fauna be somehow replicated on land? The ultimate challenge, as one of Lautenbach's colleagues would recall years later, was to determine precisely how much lime to apply per given hectare. Too little, and the buffering effect would be nil, and re-vegetation would fail to take place. Too much, and the fledgling vegetation, already stressed by the super-toxicity of the rock upon which the seeds were scattered, would be burned by the lime itself, which was a caustic.

Lautenbach and his colleagues determined to use Sudbury's sulphur-damaged landform itself as a test bed—a first there, and perhaps anywhere in the world. They began to mark off test plots on some of the most barren hills—one and a half metre-square grids were measured off and assigned numbers. Helpers were dispatched from City Hall to inspect each plot and carefully remove any sticks or stones that might hinder growth. Varying amounts of lime were assigned to each plot, and carefully recorded. The lime, mixed with a blend of plant seeds believed to be hardy enough to withstand the northern winters and high soil acidity, were scattered by hand on each plot. It was strictly low-tech stuff, but to everyone's amazement it produced almost immediate—and quite astonishing—results. When the planners arrived the following spring to inspect their test plots they found varying degrees of burgeoning plant life already apparent. It was almost miraculous, and, clearly, liming was the key. It turned out that a light dusting had produced optimum results, which was good; lime was expensive and the area requiring reclamation was vast.

But a huge challenge remained—how to apply the lime to the barren rock, some of it quite hilly and even remote—loomed over the city?

Fortunately for the City Hall bureaucrats, the new Regional Municipality of Sudbury administered not only the police and planning departments, but also the Ontario Works program, which meant it was responsible for doling out welfare cheques. Marx's "reserve army of labour" was pressed into service—in return for continued support, they were ordered to manually scatter lime and seeds over the barren Sudbury landscape.

Willingly or unwillingly, thousands of unemployed Sudburians were told to assemble en masse early in the morning before being herded onto school busses which delivered them to a preordained site somewhere high atop the black hills that loomed over the city, bulking large like the backs of so many beached whales.

And so began "the re-greening of Sudbury," an audacious scheme to re-vegetate the city's landform, and to rehabilitate its terrible public image. An aerial view of that morning would have revealed a few dozen humans moving about on the lumpy crests of the bulky black hillocks overlooking the city, interspersed with unmoving white shapes that stood out in stark relief against the black rock. These last were, in fact, bags of lime that had been spotted over the hills in roughly the proportion needed to properly neutralize the acidity in a given area.

There was some urgency to the swarm of human activity on the hilltops. Lautenbach guesstimated—

based partly on his knowledge of the region's weather patterns and partly on common sense—that there was a narrow optimal window for the scattering of lime and seed in summer, between the end of the spring rains some time in June and the start of the fall rains in August or September, either of which might wash away both seeds and lime on rock that was so bald and exposed that even the slightest precipitation could wash away the seeds before they had the chance to germinate. Indeed, severe erosion was a characteristic of Sudbury's sulphur-damaged landscape. This schedule dictated that the toiling reserve army of labour was pressed into service under the blazing heat of the July sun, which baked so much heat into the absorbent black rock that it became hot enough to melt shoe leather. These nameless, faceless individuals, who remain so to this day, are the true heroes of the Sudbury re-greening initiative, though the city's politicians (the same men who had upbraided the fiery Harry Wardell for the Sudbury MPP's blistering speeches excoriating both Inco and the provincial government for their monstrous abuse of the Sudbury environment in the first place) would all be eager enough to junket south to Rio to accept prestigious awards at the United Nations Conference on Climate and Economic Development, otherwise known as "the Earth Summit" in 1992.

By then the efforts of those anonymous toilers would come to be recognized as an unalloyed triumph of global, even epical, proportions after the following events had occurred on the black hilltops in rapid succession: the hardy, climate- and acid-resistant grasses seeded took root, creating a lush green mat that was renewed annually by the spring freshets; encouraged by this early, almost immediate, success, thousands of volunteers would fan out across the land to plant millions of trees, which would themselves seem to flourish, almost at once, creating a riotous, leafy jumble of understory that would, over the course of a few seasons grow into stately, mature shade trees.

And so, with not a small amount of human agency, the first scrubby growth Jake witnessed in that rock cut would soon see the penetration of the great Canadian Boreal Forest into the City of Sudbury, over the great rocky interstices that jutted into the urban core like so many lumpy fingers.

Following the rape of the Amazonian Rain Forest by impoverished practitioners of slash-and-burn agriculture, the Canadian Boreal had become the largest expanse of contiguous forest in the world, a vast living thing that extended in its immensity from Quebec and Ontario, through the Prairies, over the Rockies, and into the mountains of British Columbia, and it returned now into the heart of the Sudbury Basin with a vengeance, and with the orderly, stately precision of the natural world: the lesser hardwoods, more resistant to climatic and acidic stresses, came first—the coppiced birches and poplar, leggy willows, tag alder, Manitoba maple and then, gradually, the conifers—black spruce, blue spruce, cedars, and the white, red and jack-pines, which had once thickly studded the area, and whose relic stumps can still be observed in the bush even now.

Oh, but it was a marvellous thing to be a part of—to age in place—in this place, and, maturing, to witness the return of the Boreal. Spring was always the best, because you knew you were experiencing not one rebirth, but two. It was the return of green, growing things, that annual miracle, yes, but also the slow, steady advancing thing, a second, even greater miracle, the Return of the Boreal. In the whole long history of the human race, few ever get to see such a thing, the wonderful, unpredictable unexpected resiliency of Mother Nature. Because eventually that was all that it was. The human interventions—the liming, the scattering of seeds, the tree planting— was quickly outmoded by the natural order and momentum of autonomous regeneration. The seeds of the living flora were soon propagated by the small creatures who found refuge in the encroaching dense cover of the natural world. The black cap chickadees, the voles, the field mice, all advanced the Boreal and were in turn advanced by it.

But still all was not well. This was no Walt Disney World after all, for lurking unseen beneath the newly verdant veneer there still remained the most toxic residue of them all—a build-up of heavy metal depositions—mercury, cadmium, lead, mostly—that had accumulated over a century (the first ore was hoisted in Sudbury in 1885). Unlike sulphur dioxide gas, these especially nasty by-products of the nickel smelting process were emitted as particulates, or fine particles with the consistency of dust, and were not wafted thousands of miles away by the jet stream, and thus rendered harmless to the local environment. Instead, the heavy metals succumbed to the pull of gravity, falling back to earth within a few mile radius of the smelter, where they remained, in highly lethal concentrations, as a sub-soil layer beneath the lime, seeds, and grass that seemed to sugar-coat the once black rock.

As a result, the newly generated vegetation, while lovely to look at, was not at all healthy, but highly stressed, vulnerable to soil acidity, which remained high, and to the vagaries of the Sudbury climate, its short growing seasons, and, as we have seen, its brutal winters. Tissue samples of the local flora analyzed by researchers at the city's Laurentian University would confirm their worst fears—present in the roots, branches and leaves of the returning Boreal were staggeringly high levels of lethal heavy metals which had been absorbed by root systems and then travelled upward and outward to the branches and leaves of the deciduous vegetation, whose fallen leaves, composted over many years on the forest floor, would eventually decompose into humus, creating fresh, loamy topsoil that would finally bury the harmful heavy metals deeply enough that they would no longer pose a hazard. How long would this take? Generations, even many decades? No one knew, but it would have been fatuous to believe that Mother Nature, for all her marvellous resiliency could have been truly remediated from a century of greed and often-malicious neglect by simply scattering lime and a few seeds over the landscape.

A big part of the problem was, and always had been, absentee ownership. The first investors in the

Sudbury mining play had not been Canadians at all, but Americans—a brace of wealthy Cleveland industrialists who little knew—or cared—what environmental devastation their nickel smelting operation created for Sudbury and it earliest inhabitants. But when word reached Sudbury that one of the Cleveland grandees had sued an Ohio railroad company because its locomotives were belching fumes and soot over the back garden of his mansion the irony was not lost on bemused Sudburians.

In one essential for all life, at least, Sudbury's natural environment was not lacking: thanks to generous levels of annual rainfall and an abundant snowpack, fresh water was both reliable and ubiquitous. As a result, groundwater was present in copious quantities and so, absent sulphur, the Sudbury Basin's natural tendency was toward a profusion of verdure.

Surface water was present in such plenitude in the form of fresh water lakes, in fact, that Lautenbach's Planning Department once observed, only half in jest, that Sudbury was one of the few cities on earth with sufficient shore line that every household in the place could enjoy its own lake frontage.

Despite everything, however, Sudbury's blighted image was destined to linger. Its reputation as a bare-knuckled bruiser beer and hockey town would also last, even after that reality, too, had begun to fade, not least because of the titanic labour battles fought here. They weren't a revolution. But they came close, most notably for a group of strike participants whose meeting was about to get underway.

21

The Wives, Embattled

Could it be that, not so long ago, this group had indulged in a group hug?

The community organizer pondered this sorrowfully as her beloved Wives group limped into the spring. They were on the verge of splitting, acrimoniously, irrevocably. Things had gotten so bad in the meetings that she'd had to abandon the consensual approach to decision-making so dear to her. Decision-making was now, often as not, conflict resolution, and the conflicts were real, lacerating, vituperative affairs, spiteful and ugly, that threatened to split the group down the middle. As the person most often in the chair, she had watched, powerless, as things spun out of control again and again. They were all on the verge of nervous exhaustion, sick at heart by the grinding poverty of the strike, but the group's dynamic had assumed a conflictual life of its own, breaking along generational lines that pitted a more traditional woman's role against a more activist, feminist view. Whatever their ages, the community organizer knew, the cleavage stemmed from a sense of profound impotence. To the older women, perhaps, their inability to help support the family financially was a long-established matter, a social custom, almost. They had long since come to accept that their role was in the home with their husbands the principal breadwinners. But the younger women chafed under this timeworn convention, and the simmering differences broke into roiling, difficult conflict again and again. The younger women were frustrated by the absolute lack of decent work for women in the Sudbury economy. In another sense money—and the nature of the Wives' organization in relation to the Local Union—had been a flashpoint almost from the beginning of the strike, when, on a bitterly cold and windy November morning, the Wives had unilaterally decided to appear on a fundraising drive at the Falconbridge plant gates. Despite both the frostiness of the morning and the fraught historical relationship between the striking Steelworkers and the workers at Falconbridge, who had voted to remain members of the old Mine Mill Union when the Steelworkers had raided, and nearly decimated Mine Mill, the Wives were warmly greeted at the gates, and the fundraising effort had proved a roaring success.

But the problems had only started there. The Wives now had a modest treasury of their own, and their ambivalent, informal relationship with the Local 6500 Executive would become an issue. The right-wingers surrounding Jordan Nelson had never approved of the Wives. Now, here they were, going to plant gates on their own hook and raising funds in the name of the striking members of Local 6500. But who had control of the money, and where did it actually go? The conservative old guard demanded Nelson take action, which he did by indicating to the Wives that a meeting of the minds was necessary. It would have been easier for the young strike leader to delegate someone else to meet with the Wives, but that was not his way. Instead, Nelson himself ventured into the lion's den. Molly had quietly apprised him about what he was walking into: the Wives, who had raised the money through their own initiative, were in no mood to brook interference from the male-dominated Executive Board, much less to be told how to spend it, less still to share the proceeds with the Steelworkers.

Knowing the Wives were unaware of the hostility felt toward them by the old guard on his Executive, Nelson struggled manfully to express the feelings of the older, more patriarchal majority on his Executive —views he did not share—without revealing the split within his own leadership the Wives had engendered. It was wheels within wheels, and the results were predictable.

"No, Jordan! I just don't accept that we, as a group of women, should have to have our actions approved by a bunch of men!" The speaker was Arianna Murdoch, one of the more outspoken of the younger women. With her almost mannish ways and edgy assertiveness she often put off many of the older women, too.

Nelson took a deep breath, swallowed hard, and tried to remain calm. The bargaining committee had been urgently summoned to return to Toronto by the mediators, and it was vital that he put this fire out before his departure. In his absence there was no telling what could happen should the likes of Murdoch ever wind up addressing the Executive in person. Why union leaders get grey.

Jordan tried to size up the group, but other than the fact that they had listened to Murdoch with avidity and that all eyes were now turned to him, he couldn't tell what they were thinking. They awaited his response in expectant silence. "Okay, okay I get that, and we want you to know we appreciate how much the Wives have done to support the strike," Nelson began. "All we're asking is to be informed what it is you're planning to do next before it happens. No one wants to have control over your group, or its money, just some consultation, is all."

"And you promise there'll be no interference from the Local Union?"

"Yes, absolutely. We pretty much have our hands full as it is." Nelson hoped this wry understatement might draw a laugh, which it did, helping to break the ice. He began to breathe easier.

Alice McCool watched Jordan Nelson's appearance in appreciative silence, which had become her métier in the Wives' meetings of late. It wasn't that she didn't have opinions about the split opening in the organization. She did. As the group's matriarch—she was half a generation older than most of the women in the older generation side of the divide—she was pained by the looming split. But she had private worries of her own, namely the health of her daughter-in-law Jo Ann. Her pregnancy had now entered its third trimester, and Alice was concerned. Jo Ann's colour was unusually high, and her cheeks were often flushed in a way that seemed unhealthy to Alice. There were dark circles around her eyes, which gave them a hollow, haunted aspect uncharacteristic of the normally charismatic, ebullient Jo Ann.

She had sailed through the early months of the pregnancy, carrying the baby high on her slender frame, which had begun to show only later in the game. Since then the baby had dropped precipitously, causing the usual strain—and the usual pain—on her daughter-in-law's back. Jo Ann had borne all this with fortitude, rarely complaining to her mother-in-law, or as far as Alice could tell, to her son. But now it felt to Alice that everything was coming apart at the seams—the Wives, the strike dragging into yet another season—and she worried for her beautiful daughter-in-law and for the new life she carried within her. Was she getting enough sleep? Alice well remembered how uncomfortable the late stages of a pregnancy could be, especially in bed at night, with your partner fast asleep beside you, and all the natural anxieties for the future closing in, tossing and turning in fruitless, frustrating attempts to find a position comfortable enough to admit the onset of deep sleep.

She really must insist, Alice resolved, that Jo Ann go to her doctor for a routine check-up.

22

The Mad Bomber

He'd stayed now much longer than he'd intended. But the results were not what he'd hoped. Oh, the fallout from the first attack, and the blackout it triggered, had got the town buzzing, all right, and the assumption seemed to be that it was somehow related to the strike. But, apart from stretching already frazzled nerves even tighter, the hoped-for turn of public opinion against the union hadn't happened. What he hadn't reckoned for was how closely just about everyone in Sudbury was interwoven with the union. In a community of 160,000, after all, almost everyone had a neighbour or a friend or a business customer or relative among the 11,700 strikers. Conversely, the ties with the company were much more tenuous. Spook's own ties were, ironically, much closer. Langley, the Pentagon, the Wall Street law firm Sullivan and Cromwell, the former CIA head Allan Dulles, the Inco board. Not so many degrees of separation. Much of this was well above his pay grade, of course, but ours is not to reason why and Spook was nothing if not a good soldier, following each and every order with absolute, unquestioning obedience. Which was why he still lingered in this Godforsaken hellhole of a place: he'd been ordered to drive a wedge between the union and the community, and his efforts 'til now had been unavailing. And they were efforts, plural. Since blowing that first power transformer that night out on the highway, he'd done two more, each more audacious than the last. Daytime jobs in more populated areas, each closer to downtown and to the Company's operations, just in case anyone was missing the point. The most recent was a power transformer just outside the Copper Refinery building in Copper Cliff, literally just a short stone's throw away from the Refinery building itself.

While these increasingly high-risk efforts had done little to shake loose the tightly knit community of this shithole burg, they had earned him a sobriquet in the newsrooms of the city, whose reporters and assignment editors stood to attention after each and every blast. They had begun calling him "the Mad Bomber." They operated on the assumption that the series of weird events, while clearly related to each other, were linked to the strike, the rising tensions of which had become almost unbearable. Someone, doubtless a Steelworker, was ratcheting up the pressure. But so what? The police appeared to have few, if any, leads on the matter, and until charges were laid and the identity of the Mad Bomber was revealed, the bombings were strictly a sidebar story, subsumed to the main, which was the strike itself, now dragging in to its third season and two hundred fiftieth day, for those who were, like the lugubrious Jordan Nelson, counting.

23

Pit Stop

For most of the latter half of the twentieth century there was a place, just north of Parry Sound, Ontario, where Sudbury-bound Toronto travellers almost invariably stopped to break their journey, frequently encountering travellers heading the other way.

This pit stop has since been bypassed by a new, four-lane highway, and is now doubtless crumbling into a half-forgotten place of dust, rust, ghosts and scale, but on that afternoon in the spring of 1979 when Jordan Nelson and the bargaining committee pulled in on their way back up north with the ink still drying on a new, Collective Bargaining Agreement they hoped would spell an end to the ruinous, ten-month-old strike over which they were presiding, the old familiar pit stop was still a happening place.

Here they met a southbound traveller, fresh out of Sudbury.

"Hey, I know you! Ain't you Jordan Nelson?"

"Uh, yeah, that's right."

"Well, boy, I sure hope you got one helluva agreement in that there briefcase 'cause if not, the guys back home are ready to hang you right off the third floor 'a the Steel Hall!"

24

Parsing a CBA

In truth, the Agreement they brought home was a good—good enough to have averted the strike altogether back in September, perhaps even good enough to have averted the post-Thompson debacle of February—if not great, tentative Collective Bargaining Agreement. It was a standard three-year pact containing the usual wage gains. Especially important were the terms regarding the Cost of Living Adjustments, or COLA. Inflation, which could run into the double digits annually, was then a global macro-economic issue that could more than offset the annual pay increases in a new agreement. Terms of the COLA clause in the new agreement were, therefore, scrutinized more closely than the actual wage increases. Would the COLA gains of the first and second year be automatically "rolled in" to the following years, thus counting towards the overall hourly wage increase? This compounding mattered greatly to the members of Local 6500, and to the overall economy of the Sudbury community, not least because the Steelworkers at Inco had, uniquely in Canada, been able to shrewdly maintain 1961 as the base year for their COLA calculation, which skewed the calculated inflation rate very strongly in their favour. The COLA roll-in did apply in the new, tentative agreement, which the bargaining committee knew would be a strong selling point to a livid membership. The Cassandra-like pit-stop warning that had greeted Nelson only enhanced their sense of dread.

The tentative agreement was the source of much sweat and tears among the bargaining committee, whose individual members had undergone extensive solo soul-searching before voting yea or nay on whether to recommend acceptance of the deal to the membership. Each man knew what awaited him upon the group's return to Sudbury: a series of packed membership meetings in the Vimy Room, explosive tempers, and they would be facing the music on display high up on the stage above the furious, densely milling throng, not all of whose participants would necessarily be sober, or even in his right mind after ten months without cash in his pockets.

Again and again Nelson had polled them individually, one at a time, seeking unanimity as to whether the whole group would unanimously recommend acceptance of the deal. It was an agonizing, ticklish business, with each man determining his own calculus, which could—and often did—change almost overnight. Often the latest determination was announced at the end of lengthy, windy speeches that burned up the hours and left everyone feeling exhausted and drawn. Comic relief was provided by one committee member, an older Frood miner who was a popular vote-getter and holdover from Mine Mill days, much enamoured by the stentorian tones of his own perorations. In a classic on-the-one-hand-but-on-the-other-hand speech he had, over the course of a single morning, managed to declare himself both in favour of and opposed to the newly signed Memorandum of Agreement, thus earning him the everlasting private nickname "Two-Way Tom."

It was a good agreement, yes, they could all agree on that, but was it a great agreement that could even come close to approaching justification for a ten-month loss of earnings? The whole world of the Canadian labour movement was now watching the epic struggle in Sudbury. Whatever, the committee convinced itself, this was the best deal to be had at the time. They now completed the two-hour journey from the pit stop feeling no less apprehensive as to whether the membership would agree.

25

Doctor's Appointment

It happened during what was to have been a routine check-up for Jo Ann as her pregnancy entered the middle of its final trimester: the doctor fixed her with a keen, appraising look which failed to mask a measure of concern as he removed the blood pressure cuff from her arm.

"Is there a problem?"

"I'm sure not. Just a little high, is all."

She frowned, felt the first little flutter of concern. "How high?"

"160 over 90. 120 over 80 would be more like it."

"Should I be worried?"

"Oh, I'm sure not." He fixed her with a kindly smile, meant to reassure. But in his steel gray eyes over slipping bifocals she saw something else. "I suspect it's related to the fact there's so much stress out there." By which, she knew, he meant the strike.

"Your husband's out, isn't he?"

She nodded. "Yes."

He was wrapping up the thick black fabric of the BP cuff as he spoke.

"I'm sure everything's fine, but ..." he paused, almost distractedly, mid-sentence.

"Yes?"

"I'd like to refer you to an OB-gyn friend of mine, just to be on the safe side, if you don't mind ..."

"No, sure, of course, whatever you think is best," she replied with a breezy, almost off-handed confidence she did not feel.

26

Selling the CBA

The bargaining committee arrived back in town, and so began something that is, for all the civics class palaver, a rarity in our society: a true exercise in democracy. Like all such exercises it was a sweaty, sometimes dangerous affair, wildly roiling and unpredictable, despite a well-concerted attempt to contain it and to control the outcome through a five-day, time-honoured, well known dance—the selling of a new CBA. Its contents were not to be revealed publicly out of deference to the membership, who would, after all, determine its ultimate fate. The 11,700 strikers would be afforded the first glimpse of the tentative agreement's contents in a series of meetings that would be strictly private—insofar that gatherings of thousands could be private—closed door affairs off limits to the news media, where the bargaining committee would address the membership to justify their support of an agreement that might, or might not, find favour with the membership.

To that end the Steelworker brass sprang for a glossy, professionally printed, two-colour booklet, complete with charts and bar graphs, highlighting the wondrous gains made in the new agreement. But the raging thousands of hard rock miners who had been ten months without a paycheque were not about to be so easily swayed by such transparent Pittsburgh propaganda. They were inured to the union's familiar old hard-sell approach. No, this was a decision, as everyone knew, that would be hashed out in hotly-contested discussions around town over kitchen tables, in barber shops, and around taproom tables groaning with the weight of dozens of beer glasses, brimming with the foam of draft beer.

And there were staunchly vocal opponents of the new agreement who dismissed it as a "peremptory offer"—a transparent attempt by the Company to end the strike with a relatively cheap offer that featured none of the real breakthroughs that might have been expected in a strike of this duration, prominence and muscle. These naysayers tended to be the hard-core union militants, Nelson supporters mainly, skewing somewhat to the younger end of the membership. Exceptions to this demographic model were, interestingly, a handful of old school Mine Millers, still keeping the faith after all these years, for whom Jordan Nelson represented the embodiment—perhaps even the re-incarnation—of the scrappy old Local 598. The collective wisdom among these groups was, somewhat counter-intuitively, that the offer touted so robustly by the young Local Union President must be defeated to save Nelson's future in the union. Many of Nelson's closest friends and political allies in the big Local, including Molly Carruth, Jake McCool and

Foley Gilpin shared this opinion. It was necessary to destroy the village in order to save it. Acceptance of the pre-emptive offer would be a mistake of historical proportions, a repeat of the four-month 1969 strike at the height of the Vietnam War when nickel prices were soaring and the membership had voted to accept a mediocre offer, letting the Company wriggle off the hook. Foley was so convinced of this that he quietly began to play a clandestine role against his friend Nelson, secretly penning a one-page broadside against the offer. The propaganda piece was furtively passed to Jake on the steps of the Main Branch of the Sudbury Public Library on Mackenzie Street, just a block away from the Steel Hall. Jake proceeded to secretly commandeer the Local's own photocopy machine to make thousands of copies, which served to further stoke the "No" sentiments in the impending vote.

Besides the dark foreshadowing at the pit stop, the bargaining committee experienced further auguries that they were in for a rough ride. One bargaining committee member, shortly after the group's return from Toronto, had gone out for the evening with his wife. After they arrived back home he checked his phone messages and found a stark message from an anonymous male caller who warned he'd be attending the first meeting called to discuss the contract proposal, he'd be sitting in the front row, he'd be carrying a gun, and that he intended to kill as many of the sell-out members of the bargaining committee who recommended acceptance as he could. The Steel activist, one of Jordan Nelson's coterie of loyalists on the Committee, called Nelson to alert him to the threat. What else could he do?

That sort of outcome might have been averted by a chance encounter outside the Union Hall minutes before the meeting. Molly Carruth just happened to run into a worried-looking Jordan Nelson as he was heading into the Hall for the meeting. She was appalled at his attire.

"Whoah there, Jordy! Whaddaya think you're doing there, Brother?"

She eyed him up and down, taking in the business suit and tie, freshly creased pants, shiny black shoes, briefcase in hand. It was a sweltering, sunny May day. Could he really be this tone deaf?

"Jesus, Jordy, you can't go in there lookin' like a million bucks in front of a membership that ain't been paid in almost eleven months! They'll eat ya alive for sure! Better get outta that monkey suit, my friend!"

"What?" was the startled Nelson's only reaction. In working class Sudbury men donned their "monkey suits" for only two occasions: a wedding or a funeral. Only bosses dressed up in a suit and tie. Carruth's warning to Nelson may have averted his own funeral, as he quickly realized, double-timing up the stairs to his second floor office, where he hastily changed into a pair of blue jeans and casual short-sleeved shirt.

Even just hurrying across the foyer outside the Vimy Room's heavily guarded entrance doors Nelson could sense the mood of tense anticipation. The space

was thronged with latecomers who couldn't be
squeezed into the standing room at the back of the
big room. Reporters and television news crews milled
among them. The air was charged with expectancy,
as if awaiting a heavy weight prize fight. There was
a strong, palpable, sense of rancour in the building.
There would be blood.

But there were a few sweet dissidents among the
naysayers—those exceptions who would vote "no" to
the contract offer—simply because they didn't want
to go back to work. The time off agreed with them.
They were sleeping better. Their bodies had healed
from the ongoing, unnatural straining of daily labour
to produce a commodity used primarily to wreak
havoc and destruction. Now, at last, the sun was shining! The birds were singing! Sure, they missed the
money, but they felt better than they had in years.
Money, the ten-month strike had taught them, wasn't
everything. It was time to go a-fishing.

These placid few were, at best, only a tiny minority, as Jordan Nelson was about to discover as he
stepped into the roiling maelstrom of the Vimy
Room. The smell, the fetid odour of too many bodies
too tightly packed in the now summer-like heat, hit
him immediately. He swallowed once, then walked
impassively through the throng to the stage. His pas-
sage, while not unnoticed, was not obstructed. Never
in his life had he been so acutely aware of so many
eyes watching his every move. The workers in the
immediate area around him fell silent as he walked
across the vast wooden floor of the Vimy Room. The
hush was expectant, as if the silent observers antici-

199

pated that at any moment one of their number might step forward and take a poke at him, but no one did. At last he reached the short, narrow hallway to the right of the stage where, during the happier events hosted so often in this huge hall—wedding receptions, political rallies—beer was sold through a chest-high window that was shuttered now. He climbed the steps to the stage and paused again, just offstage in the wings, thinking of the anonymous death threat that had been recorded only hours before on the answering machine of one of his colleagues. He weighed the possibilities the threat was real, took another deep breath of the sweaty, stale air in the room, accentuated now because of the elevation of the stage, felt as if everything was closing in on him, decided that, on balance, there was every possibility one of the onlookers in the front row was packing a gun, squared his shoulders, and stepped out on to the stage.

27

The Wives, Divided

The new contract offer left the Wives more deeply divided than ever. The split was over two principal issues:

- Should they, as an organization that had steadily gained in profile throughout the strike, take a position on whether the tentative agreement should be accepted?
- And, if so, should they urge acceptance, or rejection?

On the first point the division tended to run along generational lines. The older women, long accustomed to the notion that their men were the breadwinners working outside the home and that their place was within it, argued strenuously that it was not women's business, that the decision was best left to the menfolk, whose votes, after all, were the only ones that really counted.

Such reasoning drove the younger women—and especially the always outspoken Molly—crazy, though Carruth was in the unique position of having a foot in both camps, even though she was no longer anyone's wife. This latter was not a point lost on any of the older women, though they were too polite to say so. For her part, Jo Ann tended to side with Molly, who only snorted derisively when one of the older women made what she, Molly, considered to be a thinly-veiled call for a return to the "barefoot and pregnant in the kitchen" days. Molly's guttural derision was not lost on the ladies of the old guard, who eyed one another with a now familiar "who let this renegade in here?" look.

It was left to Jo Ann to remonstrate. A more tractable sort than the short-tempered Molly, Jo Ann, at least, was also a stay-at-home wife wholly dependent on her husband's paycheque, like so many of the older generation. "Look, I know this is difficult," she began in what she hoped was a genial, conciliatory tone. "We're none of us used to telling our fellas what to do, right?" Her innocent, wide green eyes, filled with mischief, belied her tone, and for a moment only startled. Baffled silence greeted her words, followed quickly by a burst of appreciative laughter, an earnest that the tension that had filled the room was also bursting. But it was one thing, as they all knew, to chide their partners into a minor course of action over the kitchen table, quite another to weigh in—in public, yet—on the most important decision any of them might make in a lifetime. "But we've earned this by the way we've supported this strike through thick and thin. I know we've never done this before, but we've never been here before. A ten-month strike, and we're still standing! Who could've ever imagined such a thing? This is a new day, and a new time, for us, and for all the women in our community. Two hundred days into this thing, it's too late to turn back now! We must take a position on this offer!" Another silence greeted Jo Ann's sudden, impromptu eloquence. The traditionalists looked at each other almost sheepishly as if to determine who would offer rejoinder, but no one rose to the task.

Instead, Molly seized the moment. "Question! Madam chair, I call the question!"

The community activist, grateful that the acrimony had disappeared from the meeting for the first time in months, responded quickly. "Okay, by a show of hands, it is moved by Jo Ann McCool, seconded by Molly Carruth, that we take a public position on this offer. All those in favour ... All those opposed ..."

28

Security Detail

His hotel room phone was ringing as Cash McCallister stepped out of the shower. He'd become addicted to scalding hot showers ever since that night he'd gotten soaking wet in that goddamned icy water after he'd blown the first transformer. The weather had turned warmer now, but he just couldn't seem to shake the winter chill out of his bones. You could take the boy out of Texas, but ...

Likewise this goddamned shithole of a town. He just couldn't seem to shake it. "Yeah?" he growled into the receiver, making absolutely no attempt to disguise his foul temper.

He recognized the voice of his case officer back in Langley and simmered down a bit, intrigued almost despite himself. Very unusual to hear that voice over an open, unencrypted, line, which this was.

"Listen, we need your help up there."

"Yeah? What's up?"

"Need you on a security detail. It's urgent."

"Security detail! For who?"

"Canadian ambassador. He's there right now. Wants to meet personally with the union and the company over that strike, get a handle on what's going on. Pentagon boys are twitchier'n ever over their nickel stockpile. We need you to go with him."

McCallister rubbed his still-wet hair vigorously with a bath towel. "Huh! Why can't you just send in the Marines?" The U.S. Marine Corps, he knew, were tasked with protecting U.S. embassies, and their personnel, the world over.

"Can't. They're stuck back in Ottawa, minding the store."

"Uh huh. So whaddaya want me to do?"

"Contact Enders personally, find out his itinerary, and cover his every move when he's out in public. He's there right now. Staying at your hotel, actually."

"Yeah, well it looks like this whole situation is almost over, anyway. Union's got a new agreement and the voting on it starts any day now. Betting is they'll go for it. After ten months out on strike, how could they afford not to?"

"Well, Big Tom is there to make sure it's gonna end ASAP. Go see him, won't you, and get set to stay close 'til you can put him on a plane back to Ottawa?"

McCallister agreed to the unexpected assignment, and began to liaise with the U.S. ambassador to Canada as ordered. The only place that really concerned either man was the visit to the Union Hall, where Enders was intent on having a private sit-down with the union President and strike leader, Jordan Nelson. Neither man had spent much time inside a Union Hall and neither knew what to expect. From what Cash had observed in his few months here, the strike had become a free-for-all, and the local nickel workforce hereabouts were about as alien, unpredictable and dangerous as the Wild Men of Borneo. The two men agreed to meet again in Enders' hotel room toward the end of the week.

29

One Tough Meeting

There was no shooter in the front row, but for Jordan Nelson what came next was almost as bad,

He'd no sooner gavelled the meeting to order than a rank-and-filer none of them recognized was on his feet, approaching the stage at a run. The veins on the side of his neck were distended, and he was vituperative with rage. He seemed the very embodiment of a membership whose every hope and dream had been gashed, whose every sacrifice over that long, fraught winter had been for naught. "Nelson!" he bellowed. "Nelson! You fuckin' guy!"

"I thought you were different! I believed you'd never sell us out! But now you bring us this?" He brandished the glossy Pittsburgh propaganda leaflet over his head for all to see. "I lost my house! My wife left me! And this is all I get? Well, I say, fuck you! And fuck this shitty sell-out deal!" And with that the irate rank-and-filer retreated to his seat to a smattering of applause.

Jordan Nelson watched this outburst with apparent stoicism, at least to the casual outside observer.

But a more attentive watcher might have noticed the white-knuckle death grip with which he held either side of the wooden podium behind which he stood. At last, after clearing his throat and pausing, head down for a decent interval, the strike leader looked out over the crowd, which awaited his reply in expectant silence.

"Look, we know how much you guys have gone through out there on those lines, and my heart goes out to the Brother who just spoke, it really does. But this bargaining committee has worked hard, and brought back what we believe is the best agreement possible at this time. Believe me when I say we left nothing on the table! But now, soon, at the end of this week it'll all be up to you. And we're urging you to vote 'yes' to this agreement, to end this strike, so that you can walk back through those gates with your heads held high! Thank you!"

Nelson's words were also greeted with a smattering of applause, of roughly the same amplitude and intensity as the overwrought striker had received, a fact not lost on the members of the bargaining committee. The early auguries that the deal would be accepted were not good.

The meeting was a sweaty, over-amped four-hour grind, which Jake McCool observed from the floor. As its participants made their moody exit Jake stood his ground, awaiting the Bargaining Committee, and especially his friend, Jordan Nelson. He looked drawn, and his shoulders slumped.

"Hey Jake."

"Hi Jordy."

"So, whaddya see, whaddya hear?"

The pair stood close together, keeping their voices down, as the last few rank-and-filers left the Vimy Room.

Jake shook his head. The buzz on the floor, both inside the meeting and outside of it, had given the appearance of a membership badly divided. "Boy, I dunno, Jordy. They seem about evenly split. This deal may just not fly."

The union president gave a weary sigh and, as he turned toward the doors, it seemed to Jake, his shoulders slumped even further.

"Rough meeting, eh, Jordy?"

"Yeah, one tough meeting."

30

The Wives Take a Stand

The vote by show of hands had been so close that, much to the community organizer's exasperation, she had been unable to get a clear count. It hadn't helped that people were milling about the room.

"I'm going to need a standing vote. Everyone please stay in your seats until the vote is called!" she snapped.

No one will ever be sure of the impact Jo Ann McCool's sudden burst of eloquence had on the outcome—or on what would come later—but the standing vote revealed a razor-thin victory for the "yes" side. The Wives would take a stand on the agreement. But what would it be? Once the buzz in the aftermath of the vote count had abated, the debate over this second crucial question began in earnest. Arguments in favour of the agreement echoed sentiments heard all over town: the strike had gone on long enough—too long, in fact—and its further prolongation was more than they could bear. Besides, what was the point? The bargaining committee had unanimously recommended acceptance. Why, even the feisty Jordan Nelson had declared there was nothing more on the table, or so it was rumoured around town. Why send them back down to Toronto if there was nothing to be gained? Like Molly Carruth and her husband Jake, with whom she had discussed the matter at length, Jo Ann secretly harboured the conviction that a "yes" vote on the contract would mean the end of Jordan Nelson. He would join the long line of Sudbury strike leaders who'd failed to gain a contract that met the membership's sky-high expectations and who were summarily defeated in the next election. Like Molly and Jake—and even many of the Wives here in this room—Jo Ann had the utmost respect for the young union leader. Ergo, in order to save him it was necessary to defeat him. No one on the "no" side, as they began their impassioned perorations, disclosed this sentiment, of course. Instead were heard the usual critiques of the offer commonly heard in the coffee and barber shops—and even the hairdressers' salons—wherever strikers and their wives congregated: it was a good agreement, yes, but it certainly wasn't a great agreement worthy of a ten-month strike. So the bargaining committee had to go back down to Toronto—so what? No one knew what would transpire this time; perhaps the Company would table the great offer this time, the one it had had in its back pocket all along. And so on and so on. The arguments raged endlessly that week, destined to be resolved the only way they ever could—by the vote of the membership. And, like everyone else in the Nickel Capital that week, the Wives searched their souls and reached for the nettles ...

31

The Wives Speak Out

The Wives' debate over whether to publicly oppose the new agreement was as contentious as its predecessors, and it ran along well-worn lines. To the organization's rank-and-file members it was a question of passionate conviction. But to the community organizer presiding over it, and therefore standing somewhat detached from it, the whole thing was a wonder. How far the women in this room had come in ten short months! Many of them had never flown on a commercial airplane. Even a long distance phone call was an expensive, intimidating luxury, out of reach to most. Yet now here they were, deliberating on whether to stand at odds with the mighty Steelworkers Union, publicly breaking ranks with them for the first time.

And it was this very provincialism that galled Molly the most. The Wives who supported the contract were the Old Guard, who tended to see every question from the point of view of their kitchen, their pillow talk, their family. What was his opinion? How would he vote on the contract? His opinion was the only one that really mattered. But, as many of them realized, that ship had sailed. They were anxious, always, to declare their independence from the women's movement. The mass media had done all it could to stigmatize the early feminists, casting them as "bra burners" and "women's libbers," yet oddly here were even these most socially conservative women being drawn into a debate about doing the unthinkable. Molly had a much wider view of the strike, which had turned her world upside down. She had travelled all over the country because of it, been honoured as a labour hero, given impassioned speeches that were greeted by roaring, thunderous ovations, heady experiences she had never expected, and would never forget. She well understood the high expectations the entire Canadian labour movement had of the Sudbury strike. They were carrying the banner for everybody.

"But we're making history here," she pleaded. "We can't just give up now!" No one, she realized, argued that the agreement was worthy of all that they had gone through, only that to oppose the Bargaining Committee's unanimous endorsement was too bold, too audacious. It was the same old same old: the world is so big and we are so small, stay as we are. "What about all those smaller unions out there?" she demanded. "They look up to us, and if we accept this agreement it'll look like a defeat, and they'll say, 'If they couldn't do it, then what's the point in us takin' the bosses on?'" Molly paused to give her words a chance to sink in. This time, it was Jo Ann who rushed into the breach. "Question! Madam Chairperson, I call the question!" Jo Ann knew, as they all did, how heart-ily sick everyone in the room was of these endless, debilitating debates. The call to a vote came almost as a relief. The community organizer briefly recapped the gist of the resolution on the floor: they would issue a press release announcing that WSS (their organization had now evolved to the highest, most-established org-order, the acronymic) had decided it could not support the Tentative Agreement. This did not mean, however, they no longer supported the Bargaining Committee, Local 6500, or the strike itself, only that this particular agreement was unworthy of such a lengthy strike. They believed the Bargaining Committee could do better, and they urged the Committee to return to the bar-gaining table and consolidate their gains.

The motion carried by a narrow margin. So what happened now? The community organizer took charge, and began to issue a stream of orders: they were at the eleventh hour, and the voting would begin in the morning. If their news release was to have any impact on the outcome, it must go out to the local news media right away. Would someone please get it typed up and photocopied? Oh, and there was one other thing; they should notify Jordan Nelson of their decision before it went to the media. They owed the man that much, at least. No one was especially anxious to break the news to the fiery union leader, but Arianna Murdock, of all people, drew the short straw. She was at pains to break the news to him as gently as possible.

"Because it just isn't good enough after eight months, Jordy ..."

"Last fall it would have been enough ..."

"Maybe if you hadn'a called it such a great agreement in the meeting ..."

In the end they simply agreed to disagree and Arianna rang off.

Jordan Nelson was alone when the call came in on this, quite possibly, last night of the strike. It just seemed fitting to him that he spend the evening at home, alone, away from the buzz of the second floor, the incessant ringing of the telephones.

He hung up the phone call from the Wives, swirled the ice around in his drink, and contemplated the morrow.

Whatever the outcome, he was certain of this much: nothing would ever be quite the same ever again.

32

Interlude

At some point that night, as the city slept, fitfully, and as Jordan Nelson contemplated his drink, morosely, this also happened, unbeknownst to almost everyone: in the granite fastness and in the stopes, drifts and cross-cuts that honeycombed the rock beneath the city's streets an unfamiliar sound was heard for the first time in many months—the cranking over of a thousand scoop tram engines, and the steady, pulsing thrum of nearly as many diesel engines idling.

So certain was the Company of the vote's outcome—so desperate was the thirst for a swift return to full production—that senior management ordered shift bosses to travel underground to warm up the scoops, many of which, it was assumed, would have dead batteries after ten months of inactivity.

The Company was right about its machines, wrong about its workers. It certainly seemed a safe enough bet; how could anyone in his right mind vote against a return to a steady paycheque in the face of utter destitution? If the senior managers and directors of

Inco understood anything about human nature it was the sturdiness and absolute reliability of that greatest of human motivators: greed.

It had been deployed with fabulous success, after all, in the Sudbury mines for nearly a century. The individual mine production bonus, wherein a man's labour was incentivized to drive him to drill, blast, and drill again without supervision, had produced billions upon billions in profits. The donkey trotted dutifully after the dangling carrot. It had always worked before. Men would drive themselves beyond the point of exhaustion, tempt the fates, cut corners on safety, venture beneath that corner of sketchy, unbolted ground, to put that extra penny in the pay packet.

Why should tomorrow be any different? Surely, it would not.

And so, as an entire city tossed and turned in fitful, uneasy slumber the engines of production, revived, idled steadily on, awaiting the still-absent essential, the necessary and final steady beating heart of the thing: human labour power.

33

Southwind on the Move

Acting Lieutenant Curtis Southwind heaved yet another monumental sigh as he turned over yet another page from the file. The pages had been perused so often they were becoming dog-eared. The passenger manifests had yielded nothing, working backward from arrivals at YSB to the hub of the Toronto International Airport, usually, and then backwards from there to the point of origin. He was missing something, but what was it? He'd pinpointed perhaps a half-dozen potential suspects, all engineers, but they all appeared to be on legit business trips to one of the two big nickel companies in the city. They possessed all the requisite skill sets to wreak the kind of damage he'd seen at the transformer station. But why would a Company man sabotage his own property? The only reason he could think of was to discredit the union, but that was a risky gambit— committing a felony to prove a dubious point. If he cracked this case, brought a Company manager up on charges, it would be game over for the Company in the strike. No, such a clandestine strategy was too risky for Inco. Maybe it really was the union. If it walked like a duck ...

With another, even more monumental sigh Southwind heaved his not inconsiderable bulk out of his desk chair.

"Gonna leave the building for awhile," he informed a subordinate at an adjacent cubicle. CIB was crammed in like sardines up here on the second floor of the cop shop.

"Oh yeah? Where ya goin', sir?"

"Over t' the union hall. Think mebbe it's time I had a little talk with them fellas."

34

History Is Made at the Steel Hall

Parking was impossible at the Steel Hall, forcing Southwind to park far down Frood Road, almost to the Moose Lodge, which forced the police lieutenant to trudge two blocks back in the surprisingly warm early spring heat. Already frustrated by his fruitless pursuit of the Mad Bomber, Southwind was badly winded, and grumpier than ever, as he ascended the cement steps leading to the main floor of the Steel Hall.

The joint was jumping with rank-and-file union members buzzing in and out, eager to cast their vote on the proposed contract and then to get on with their day. The big man in the dark suit shouldered his way gruffly through the loosely milling throng, only to find himself confronted by yet another set of stairs.

The buzz in the floor above was palpable, the air thick with cigarette smoke, tension, and the incessant ringing of telephones. No, Jordan Nelson could not possibly see him, the union president was far too busy. Nonplussed, Southwind worked his way through the roster of the big Local's Executive Board until he eventually was escorted into the office of Local 6500 Vice President Jake McCool.

"Jake? This is Lieutenant Southwind, Sudbury Regional Police." Angel Houle escorted the burly cop into Jake's office.

"Acting Lieutenant," Southwind corrected.

Jake looked up, intrigued, saw a big man, slow moving, eyes so heavily lidded he could have been mistaken for semi-somnolent, or even dim-witted.

Jake motioned at the chair facing his desk. Southwind took it, gratefully, missing nothing. How many times had he done this? Sizing up a stranger who was also instantly, a suspect? Hoping that stranger would be disarmed by his appearance even as he remained alert to all the little tells of dissembling. The slightest tic, blink, eye movement, spoke volumes.

But Southwind felt none of this from the young union man, found only an openness, and fresh curiosity. As was his wont, Southwind had come straight to the point with the Union Vice President, explaining the baffling case of the search for the Mad Bomber. McCool evinced a keen, alert interest in the matter which even Southwind, old jade, product of an ancient, ancient civilization, felt was genuine. McCool seemed to take it as a given that such blatant anti-Company sabotage was some kind of set-up intended to discredit the union. But then, what else would he say?

"So then, you have no idea who might have done this?"

"No. No idea at all." He never missed a beat. Even if he hadn't done it, the kid would have heard something. This frickin' Union Hall was like one giant ant heap.

The two men then slipped into an easy, apparently casual conversation when McCool suddenly stiffened, and stopped talking mid-sentence. "I uh, I— sorry, what were we talking about?" The colour had drained from McCool's face.

Southwind, instantly alert, paused for a beat, listening to the commotion outside the office. The walls were thin and did not extend quite all the way to the ceiling, so the adjacent, incessant hub-bub was clearly audible. There it was again, a man's voice, rising in barely suppressed anger, a southern twang "Look. Maybe you-all didn't hear me straight the first time! I said Mr. Thomas Enders is here to see Jordan Nelson!"

McCool, suddenly, looked white as a sheet. "I-I know that voice!" He spoke in a whisper. Southwind sensed that he had instantly become some kind of confidant, being beseeched by someone who was terrified of— something. Jake, still in a whisper, quickly stammered out a quick story about his brother Ben, how he'd been beaten to death in a back-alley altercation with a mysterious stranger outside the Hotel Coulson, and how the stranger had vanished. He hadn't ever really seen the assailant, but had heard his voice more than once.

Southwind's skin began to crawl. "And you're sure that's it? That's the voice you heard?"

Jake nodded. His face wore a look of wide-eyed wonder, but he rose to his feet swiftly, emerged from behind his desk, headed for the door.

To Jake's surprise Southwind moved even faster—with a grace astonishing for such a big man—heading him off at the door. The cop laid a mitt on Jake's shoulder and squeezed it once in what he hoped would be read as a reassuring gesture. "Now why don't you let me handle this?" he said softly.

They emerged from the office together, scanning the waiting area outside Jordan Nelson's office. As usual, all the seats there were taken. Their gaze fell at once on a bearded man of indeterminate age slouching in a chair, long legs splayed out in front of him, as if he owned the place. He radiated an aura of pure, insolent arrogance.

"Is that the man?" Southwind asked Jake.

"He looks different, but yes, that could be him."

As they approached the lounging stranger, Southwind felt the hair on the back of his neck begin to rise. Creepy morning 'round the old Steel Hall. But he had learned long ago to trust the primal above all.

At that moment another stranger emerged from inside another union office, odd looking bird wearing eyeglasses with thick lenses on an oversized, balding head. Like young McCool, he, too, looked like he'd just seen—or rather, heard—a ghost. Southwind watched in silence as he exchanged a silent, knowing, glance with McCool.

The stranger saw them coming, and grunted a greeting of sorts at Southwind, still in the lead. "Mornin', Chief. Somethin' I can do for you?"

McCool shot a quizzical glance at the bespectacled stranger, who gave a single, emphatic nod. Only much later, in the course of his subsequent investigation, would Southwind learn the significance of those knowing looks: McCool and the other man, who would identify himself as Foley Gilpin, were the only two living souls in Sudbury who could identify this suspect. The southern U.S. accent was the giveaway, the distinctive voice that had carried through a closed hotel room door on a long ago morning when Gilpin and McCool, on the trail of Ben McCool's killer, had gone bursting in only to discover Jo Ann's father, a high-ranking Inco executive, sitting with him, a heart-stopping revelation that had sent the stunned Jake McCool reeling backward out the hotel room door with Gilpin following in hot, bewildered pursuit. Not the strongest eyewitness ID he'd ever known, but the moment had left such an indelible impression on both men that Southwind would deem it credible, even after all these years.

Southwind flashed his badge wallet. "You can stand up when I'm talking to you, for starters."

The stranger smirked, but did as he was told.

"Okay, pal, now put your hands behind your back, turn around, and spread 'em."

Once again the stranger complied, but now the smirk was gone.

Southwind had nearly completed his pat-down when he felt something around the right ankle. Pulling up the pant leg, he found a leather holster, well worn but clearly top grain cowhide, obviously custom made. Strapped inside was a small knife, a lovely lethal little piece with a finely balanced heft in Southwind's hand. He flipped it open. The blade had been worn down by repeated sharpenings over the years, but there was no doubting it was honed to a razor's edge. Southwind flipped it closed, returned it to the holster, and stood up with a heavy grunt.

"Well, my friend, I'm arresting you for carrying a concealed weapon, and much else, including suspicion of murder."

At these words a tall man in an expensively tailored suit accosted Southwind. He towered over the rest of them, and he was sputtering a protest as he approached.

"What is going on here? This man has committed no crime! I demand you release him at once!"

Southwind turned. "And you are?"

"Enders. Ambassador Thomas Enders. I am the Ambassador of the United States to this country, and this man is assigned to my security detail. And, as such, I am certain he enjoys diplomatic immunity in your country."

"Not for murder, he doesn't," Southwind replied grimly.

"Murder! Why, that's preposterous! And just when ... You've never even been in this city before, have you, McCallister?"

Southwind, who had kept the perp's wrists tightly pinioned in one hand, turned him around so they could all see his face. He only shrugged in answer to the question, hesitated, and looked at the floor. Although it lasted only a split second, the pause was all any of them needed to know.

"And not only that, Mr. Ambassador, your man is carrying an illegally-concealed weapon in my jurisdiction. Now I'm going to give you the benefit of the doubt here and assume you knew nothing about it ..."

Enders, clearly flustered, threw his hands in the air, and turned away.

The mini-drama that played out on the second floor of the Steel Hall that day would pass largely unnoticed, subsumed by the much larger drama that would play out one floor below a few hours later, when the results of the ratification vote were announced: in a stunning decision that would make front page headlines across the nation, the members of Local 6500 had voted fifty-six per cent against the proposed agreement.

As news of the results spread across the Sudbury Basin, dozens of strikers converged on 92 Frood Road for a joyous victory celebration in the downstairs taproom, Jake and Jo Ann McCool, Molly Carruth, and Foley Gilpin among them.

Also sitting at the long table, fairly groaning beneath the weight of so many brimming draft beer glasses, sat Jordan Nelson's many enemies within the union, grim-faced. They had never really approved of the brash young union leader, had counted on an acceptance vote to be his death knell. Now, it was the union militants' turn to exult, and, on this one night at least, it felt as if the earth had opened up beneath the feet of the old, Cold Warrior guard. "Oh, mama, could this really be the end? To be stuck outside of Hanmer with the Sudb'ry blues again ..."

35

Thirty and Out

Despite the fact they were both nursing mild hang-overs and it was a Sunday, both Jordan Nelson and Jake McCool showed up at the deserted union hall the day after the big vote. Nelson, to clear up some last-minute paperwork before his departure back down to Toronto, Jake to check in with his picket captains to assess the mood out on the lines. (The response: morale was high, everyone excited to see what would come next.)

But what *would* come next? The question was top-of-mind with Nelson, who dropped into Jake's office for a casual chat.

"Hey, Jake, you were at Frood after me, right?"

Jake shrugged in assent.

"Was Charley Burrell still there?"

"Old guy who'd be so tired at the end of his shift he had to sit down in the shower above the drain? Yeah, sure, everyone knew Charley." And every Frood miner had known his story, which had become a legend: how Charley had begun his career at Frood Mine in the Dirty Thirties with a spectacular year of bonus earnings, amassing a small fortune in the process. Hoping to become richer still, Charley had invested heavily in the local real estate market, which had collapsed shortly after, along with the world nickel price, wiping Charley out. But Charley, certain that his luck would turn, refused to bow to fate. For years—decades, even—Charley busted his butt to earn big bonus, long after his youth, and his strength, were spent. But the magic was gone, and Charley's glory days never returned. Most of his peers had long since retired, but Charley soldiered stubbornly on, afflicted by the deafness, arthritis, and White Hand Syndrome so common among old jackleg miners. By Jake and Jordan's time, Charley had become an old, old man, haunted by a dream of one more year of fabulous bonus earnings. Just one. And so Charley had become a familiar, pathetic sight, sitting on the floor of the shower in the Frood Mine dry, sluicing himself in the grey water running off the filthy bodies of a hundred of his compatriots.

Both men paused to contemplate Burrell's life story, the arc of it. "Ya know, I've been thinking of Charley a lot lately," Jordan said at last.

"Yeah? How so?"

Jordan drew a deep breath. "I think it's time we went balls-in for thirty and out."

"Huh!" Jake was momentarily stunned that the union president was seriously contemplating going for the gusto when it came to the Holy Grail of collective bargaining in Canadian heavy industry, but it made sense. The stipulation that any worker could take his or her full pension after thirty years' service regardless of age had long been a prized, though elusive, goal in bargaining. The removal of the "age factor" combined with years of service would remove a common barrier to retirement eligibility for many. Such a breakthrough, precedent-setting concession by the company would, in all likelihood, seal the deal. It would be difficult for the rank-and-file to reject that.

"Do you really think the Company would go for it?"

"Well, they want us back on the job pretty bad. If we tell them that's what it's gonna take to get us back to work ... "

"Betcha old Charley still won't take it," Jake grinned.

Nelson sighed. "Oh, I know, and there's lots more like him. But at least they'd have the choice ..." The union president chose not to voice the obvious, knowing it was an article of faith among the union activists throughout the big Local: thirty years of service in a hostile, often lethal, working environment like a hard rock mine was enough for anybody, and in the name of simple human decency should be rewarded with a full, liveable pension, regardless of age.

"Well, brother, more power to ya, and to the whole Bargaining Committee."

"Yeah, thanks, Jake."

And with that the union president closed up his office, descended the stairs to the back door, and headed back down the road to Toronto. The strike had just entered its two hundred fiftieth day.

36

261

The Bargaining Committee returned, triumphant, just six days later. They had won a package that did include thirty and out, plus full Cost-of-Living-Adjustment roll-ins, wage increases in each of the three years of the agreement, and some improvements to contract language that would help the stewards police the agreement on the job. There was nothing not to like, and the bargaining committee, which was once again unanimous in urging acceptance, breezed through the membership meetings, which were pacific affairs in comparison to the stormy meetings of the previous go-round. Everyone sensed that the strike was winding down, and the vote to ratify was carried by a wide margin.

It was over. A ten-and-a-half month strike, two hundred sixty-one days, to be precise. Although it had been settled on the union's terms, there was no celebration, no bust-up. Instead, everyone felt numb and more than a little bewildered. So, they would return to work. (More than a few felt better of it, choosing to book holidays instead, which drove the

Company's HR people over a cliff. Here they were, rushing to resume full production, and these crazy men, after ten months off the job, wanted to take a vacation?)

But mainly this new normal, which really was nothing more than a return to the old, familiar, albeit now half-forgotten, normal, was bewildering. What would happen to the clothing exchange, the food bank, the Scrounge Committee? It all felt strange, more than a little surreal. It would take days for the embattled rank-and-file before relaxation could seep in. Meanwhile, life moved on ...

... It was Alice McCool who had insisted her son accompany Jo Ann to her ultrasound appointment.

In private, though never to her face, Alice had begun to refer to her daughter-in-law as "that poor girl." An only child whose parents had passed on years earlier, Jo Ann had no family, especially in comparison to the prolific, roistering McCool clan who surrounded Alice and her husband Big Bill at every birthday and holiday.

Alice certainly never meant it in any sort of patronizing way—to the contrary, she idolized Jo Ann, never more than in those memorable moments when she and Molly Carruth, through their impassioned, quick thinking imprecations had carried the day, persuading a majority of the reluctant Wives to come out publicly against that first offer. 'Til her dying day Alice McCool would remain convinced that the Wives, public stand against the first, peremptory offer had swung the vote decisively. How appropriate. From counselling acceptance in the bitter, ruinous strike of '58 to leading a proud, stubborn resolution to fight on in the strike of '78, resulting in a pure, unalloyed union victory. The Wives had surely atoned. But it was because they had known their own history, and learned from it, as Alice knew all too well. Still the McCool matriarch worried about her daughter-in-law's first-ever pregnancy while she nervously awaited a call as to the outcome.

So Jake was with Jo Ann in the darkened ultrasound room as the apprehensive mother-to-be lay flat on her back, big belly exposed, covered in some cold, oily-feeling goo as the ultrasound tech rolled a small wand over her belly, accompanied by strange, squishy sounds out of a loudspeaker mounted beneath a screen which the operator studied intently.

After what seemed an eternity she turned, smiling, toward the young couple. "Everything looks fine, just fine. Congratulations."

"C-Can you tell us when I'm likely to deliver?" Jo Ann wondered aloud, anxiety clearly evident in her voice.

But the ultrasound tech only shook her head. "Afraid not. That's pretty chancy, always. You're in your third trimester, that's for sure, but beyond that, unless we know the exact date of conception, which few couples ever do …"

Jo Ann and Jake looked at each other, and blushed slightly.

"Uh, actually we do know," Jake offered. "It was exactly 261 days ago." He thought of the long, apprehension-filled night before the strike had started. It seemed another lifetime.

The ultrasound tech returned her tool to Jo Ann's belly, and rolled it around some more.

She turned to them again, wiping the goo off the sensor. "And have you figured out a name yet for your little boy?"

This was unexpected. Jo Ann looked up at Jake, and was surprised to find him a bit misty-eyed.

He nodded once, and all he said was, "Bill."

Thank you to Cathy Mulroy for sharing her stories from
her own memoir book "My View from Blacken Rocks."
The character of Molly was inspired by real life events that
occurred during the 1978/79 strike in Sudbury, Steelworkers
6500 vs INCO. Thanks also David Patterson for his help.

Without their help and that of many others, this work of
fiction would never have been able to capture the nature
and temperament of the strike from beginning to end.

MORE FROM BARAKA BOOKS

The Nickel Range Trilogy
Volume 1 - The Raids
Volume 2 – The Insatiable Maw
Mick Lowe

A Beckoning War
Matthew Murphy

Speaks to Me in Indian
David Gidmark

The Adventures of Radisson
Volume 1 – Hell Never Burns
Volume 2 – Back to the New World
Volume 3 – The Incredible Escape
Martin Fournier

Songs Upon the Rivers
The Buried History of the French-speaking Canadiens *and Métis*
From the Great Lakes and the Mississippi across to the Pacific
Robert Foxcurran, Michel Bouchard, and Sébastien Malette

Rebel Priest in the Time of Tyrants
Mission to Haiti, Ecuador and Chile
Claude Lacaille

Washington's Long War on Syria
Stephen Gowans

Scandinavian Common Sense
Policies to Tackle Social Inequalities in Health
Marie-France Raynault & Dominique Côté

America's Gift
What the World Owes to the America's
and their First Inhabitants
Käthe Roth & Denis Vaugeois

Printed in April 2017
by Gauvin Press,
Gatineau, Québec